MISS SEETON GETS IN ON THE ACTION

"C'mon." The taller man grabbed Miss Seeton's arm. "In the car quick or I'll do yer."

"I think," said Miss Seeton, drawing herself up so that she reached nearly to his shoulder, "that you must have made a mistake."

A short man rushed at her escort, Officer Tom Haley. Haley performed a high kick that would have secured him a place in any chorus line, came down astride his adversary's neck, scissored the man's head in an attempt to keep his seat and rode his unwilling charger down into the back of Miss Seeton's assailant.

Lofty was first on his feet. Shorty had had it, by the looks. He saw Tom Haley sprawled on hands and knees, trying to rise. Easy. He let the cosh drop from his sleeve on its wrist thong and raised it above Haley's head.

Miss Seeton realized his intent. "Stop that!" she commanded. Instinctively she slapped her handbag against his head; the gilt bird's-claw clasp ripped his temple, he yowled, and the bag burst open, showering the combatants with some three thousand pounds.

ODDS ON MISS SEETON
HERON CARVIC

BERKLEY BOOKS, NEW YORK

This Berkley book contains the complete
text of the original hardcover edition.
It has been completely reset in a typeface
designed for easy reading and was printed
from new film.

ODDS ON MISS SEETON

A Berkley Book / published by arrangement with
the author's estate

PRINTING HISTORY
Peter Davies edition published 1975
Berkley edition / January 1989

ISBN: 0-425-11307-8

A BERKLEY BOOK ® TM 757,375
Berkley Books are published by The Berkley Publishing Group,
200 Madison Avenue, New York, New York 10016.
The name "BERKLEY" and the "B" logo
are trademarks belonging to Berkley Publishing Corporation.

PRINTED IN THE UNITED STATES OF AMERICA

10 9 8 7 6 5 4 3 2 1

For
Phyllis
as is all I do

ODDS ON MISS SEETON

chapter

~1~

SHE WAS BACK, still alone, perched on a stool at the end of the bar.

The younger of the two barmen poured a drink, set it in front of her and leaned forward to light a cigarette. The girl took time to inhale and to emit a stream of smoke, the deliberate movements of her hands advertising relaxation and control.

A middle-aged man who had begun by facing her during her previous appearance there now lolled, glass in hand, with his back pointedly turned.

A man in his thirties approached, spoke to the barman, then leaned on the counter eying the girl, but within a minute he too had swung round and, hitching himself onto a stool, ignored her.

Why? the young man who was watching her from a distance at a supper table for two wondered. A shill? Experience accepted the likelihood, but feeling rebelled. If she was, she certainly must be saving her come-on for someone special. You'd've thought a girl on her tod at a bar'd be fair game, but the way she'd choked off those two types—though from here he couldn't see how she'd done it—it looked like she wasn't in the game at all, and both of them were now obviously appeasing their egos with huff and sour grapes. He'd never really liked women in trouser suits, but somehow on her . . . That black material with gold in it and an occasional splodge of roses suited her— suited the place—or something.

He studied those expressive hands as she talked to the barman: right elbow on the counter, first finger pointed, while the other fingers and the thumb flexed and weaved in counterpoint. Under cover of the tablecloth he tried the movement out himself. No go. His forefinger refused to remain static and insisted on fraternizing with the chorus. He brought his hand up in quick embarrassment when the waiter arrived to replenish the glasses.

"Champagne for the lady, and for you, sir"—his tone bordered on a sneer—"ginger beer. And you prefer to add your own gin?"

A nodded assent. The waiter retreated and the young man surreptitiously switched glasses with the elderly woman who was his companion, lifted the gin bottle from the table, added a measure to the champagne and controlled a grimace as he sipped the result. He concentrated again on the girl.

The hands were still at it. The cigarette was put out, a quarter smoked, a new one drawn from a silver—platinum?—case was lit by the barman, her glass was raised, sipped, set down, and during her entire conversation with the barman the hands were in play. They say English people don't use their hands while talking. Not true; hell of a lot of 'em did, but he'd never seen anybody use 'em like this girl, in a constant, flowing, slow, graceful, unconscious— Uhuh; not so damned unconscious. Ash had fallen on her lap. The left hand made a quick dart, was arrested in midmotion and then continued the gesture as a languid brush-off.

The waiter returned to remove the plates. He eyed a half-eaten portion of sole Walewska.

"You've finished, sir?"

The young man roused himself. "What? Yes—and hold

the next course a bit while we have another go at the tables."

"Very good, sir."

Realizing that he had been remiss in his attention to his companion, the young man sprang to his feet, seized her handbag and pulled back her chair.

Shrugging, the waiter watched their departure for the roulette tables. People. The next course was ready. Well, it could sit and stew till they'd lost enough lolly to take interest in their nosh again. Though, come to that, he'd heard the last time she'd staked, the old bag'd made a killing. He looked askance at the gin bottle on the table; glanced at the ice bucket, where champagne was nuzzled by ginger beer as though the wine bottle had pupped after slumming. He shrugged again. People. And that young pimp needed to watch his step or there'd be trouble—sitting there pushing his food around, all gooey-eyed over that pint at the bar and not so much as a how's-your-auntie to the old tart he was mealing with and who'd be paying the dibs. She'd blow her wig before they were through, you'd see. Look, chum, he mentally apostrophized the absent young man. Look where the lolly is—three strings of sparklers round that stringy neck and enough on her fingers to make knuckledusters. So take on a job—if you'd call it that—and see it through without whoring after pints at bars.

The girl at the bar waited until the elderly woman accompanied by the young man had passed, then, stubbing out her cigarette and leaving her barely tasted drink, she slid from her stool and followed them.

"Les jeux sont faits?"

The girl had stationed herself behind the chair of the elderly, overpainted woman. She leaned forward and with a quick, nervous gesture placed a chip on the square marked 31, where it rubbed edges with the single counter already resting there. She straightened and composed her face to a mask of indifference.

The croupier spun the wheel.

"Rien ne va plus."

Expressionless faces watched the jumping, clicking ball and only the table's surface could read the avarice, the hope or fear in the eyes beneath lowered lids. The wheel slowed, the clicks became less frequent and the ivory ball dropped into the slot numbered 14, rose on the ridge which separated it from the neighboring compartment, fell back, only to rise again and topple as though exhausted into the space next door. Less than a sigh, a mere susurration of breath greeted the result.

"Trente-et-un, noir et impair," remarked the croupier, and his indifferent rake swept up and down, collecting the majority of stakes, then paid assorted winners the single dues to the few bets on black, on high and on uneven numbers and the double obligations to those on the correct dozen or column, and finally pushed two piles of thirty-five *jetons,* already stacked by one of the assitant croupiers, down the length of the table to where the two chips on 31 awaited them.

Maintaining her air of boredom, the girl collected her gains, although a tremor in her hands betrayed her and her fingers fumbled the chips. Two rolled from the table to the floor. The young man in attendance behind the elderly woman's chair dived and retrieved them, to be rewarded with a curt "Thanks." He reached for his companion's winnings, took her handbag, slipped them in and held it for her as she rose from her seat.

The girl was prepared to take the vacant chair, but stopped for a moment to watch the couple move back down the length of the immense room toward the curved steps that led to the raised level where the supper tables were set.

Disgusting. He was young enough to be that old woman's son—grandson. Even if he didn't look the type, he was still nothing better than a ponce dancing to the tune of a painted hag. By the time she turned back to the table, the chair was occupied. A middle-aged woman in a shapeless coat and a felt pudding bowl for a hat, which if it had ever had a shape had long since lost it, was already seated, engrossed with paper and pencil in calculations concerning the run of the numbers and the frequency of red versus black.

"Mesdames et messieurs, faites vos jeux."

The girl hesitated. Carry on while her luck was in? No. It wasn't hers—she'd only followed the lead of that old trout. Besides, if Fortune smiled you had to thank her or she deserted you. Without waiting for the result of the next spin, she walked slowly in the wake of the older woman and her escort.

Free from the stimulus of the roulette wheel, she found the atmosphere of the place oppressive. The name The Gold Fish had fired but one spark in the imagination of an interior decorator and he had repeated the motif mercilessly throughout the casino. Occasional encircled fish were woven in shades of orange and brown into the deep gold pile of the carpet and the yellow brocade upholstery of the chairs and sofas, while fish in shoals swam coyly in and out of the folds of curtains. Plaster casts of fish, duly gilded, appeared above doorways, on the ceiling and in panels around the walls, giving the impression of copper molds in some gargantuan kitchen. The glittering drops of the chandeliers and wall brackets proved on inspection to be topaz-colored fish hanging in clusters like the catch of anglers who had ignored the rule that they should throw back the undersized. Finally, in case the point should have been missed, glass fronts of tanks glowed in false sunlight on the wall space between the panels to display the languorous movements of such tropical marine species as could boast the correct coloring.

The girl reached the steps to the supper enclave with the feeling that she was wading ashore on some South Sea island, and the young man jumped to his feet as he noticed her approach, gripping the back of his chair to steady himself.

"Thank you for rescuing my two chips," said the girl.

"Not a bit," he protested. "Easy to drop those counter things. Congratulations on your win."

"Actually," she replied, "I came to thank your"—her upper lip curled—"your friend."

The waiter, with a blank expression more effective than a sneer, came forward with another chair, set an extra glass

and poured champagne for the two women, ginger beer for
the young man, then turning to the trolley behind him, he
lifted the waiting crêpes de volaille into the pan on the spirit
stove, poured kirsch and flared them. The distraction of the
flame did not prevent the girl from seeing the young man
quickly switch glasses with his companion and then
ostentatiously add gin to his champagne. She looked at him
with contempt.

"I'm not staying."

"Oh, but you must."

"Must?"

"Yes, of course," he insisted. "You must drink to
celebrate your luck."

"I should hate," she retorted, "to deprive you. I'm sure
you could manage the extra glass and you can always top
it—" She stopped. From under the mascaraed fringe of
false eyelashes, the eyes of the older woman were weighing
her. In spite of the vulgarity, the outrageous makeup, the
obsessive dazzle of sequins, the excessive clutter of
diamonds at ears, throat, wrists and hands, the woman's
steady regard made the girl feel foolish. She felt like a child
indulging in a tantrum and recognized that temper had led
her to the verge of inexcusable bad manners. Her hands
rose, the fingers sketched an apology, described an arc of
resignation and she sat.

"Of course you must," the young man repeated. "You
must always celebrate your luck."

"It wasn't mine, it was . . ." She glanced at the other
woman and floundered.

"Sorry." He grinned. "Mrs. Amos B. Herrington-Casey,
Tom Haley . . ." He looked at the girl inquiringly as he
took his seat and the waiter began to serve.

The girl ignored the implied question. "I'm sorry, Mrs.
Herrington-Casey. I only came to thank you because I
followed your play and won. If you don't give thanks
for luck it deserts you—or that's what they say. Silly,
I suppose, but it was the first time I'd won anything
and . . ." Her hands upturned and the fingers finished
the sentence.

The magenta lips of the older woman stretched in a smile. "It comes, I think, from an ancient superstition that if you claim gifts from the gods for your own, they will take their revenge—the gods, I mean—and reclaim them. The gifts, that is to say."

The girl stared. The voice was so different from what she'd expected: harsh, and probably American from the name. But this voice was somehow out of place: calm, earnest, like—more like a schoolteacher. There was something about this old girl—something offbeat. Something about this Tom Haley—something that didn't match up.

"Well." She raised her glass in a toast and sipped. "Thanks anyway." She started to rise.

"Wait," commanded the young man. "You can't leave without finishing your champagne. I'm sure that'd be bad luck. Have something to eat. We'll be playing again when we've finished this course—won't you, Mrs. H.-C.?" His companion nodded. "Then you can follow up this luck of yours."

There was, he thought, something about this girl—something off-key—something . . . Why had she dodged giving her name? Tom Haley flattered himself that he was analyzing the situation professionally, viewing her dispassionately; unaware that he was gazing at her with all the infatuation of a moon-struck calf.

"Haley?" Detective Chief Superintendent Delphick frowned. "Wasn't he the D.C. you had on duty at Heathrow when Miss Seeton went to Switzerland?"

Inspector Borden of Fraud chuckled. "Yes, Oracle, and, too, when she came back armed with an arm."

At his desk on the other side of the office, Delphick's assistant, Sergeant Ranger, flinched. He preferred to forget the episode of Miss Seeton's return from abroad, with her declaration to customs of a wedding present for Anne and himself and the resultant commotion when the stainless steel platter proved to have a plastic-wrapped human arm lying on it. And, as late in the day as this and wanting his dinner, and only just back with the Oracle from their jaunt to Middlesborough, and typing up the reports on it, he'd just as soon forget Miss Seeton—or Aunt Em, as she had now become to Anne and himself—altogether. Anyway, Fraud must be off their tots to think of using her again after that shemozzle abroad. Even the Oracle, who understood her better than most, couldn't always control her—and sure as hell nobody else could. It wasn't, he supposed, her fault if somebody stuck odd pieces of bods in her luggage, but it was still the sort of thing that happened whenever she was let loose. It was off enough having her attached to the force at all, but it was off to ask her to do anything more than the odd drawing or so when wanted.

". . . and someone," Borden was saying, "who can draw a recognizable likeness from memory is what we want."

"You've tried photos?" asked Delphick.

"No go. We sent a man in with a candid camera, but the film turned up blank. They're using a ray same as they do at airports. There's nothing actually illegal about it and anyhow they'd justify it by saying they were checking that no one gets into the casino with any hardware, but they know damn well it scrubs all film too. So there you are. Your Miss Seeton—our MissEss—is the answer."

Delphick was dubious. "See your point, but couldn't she have been slipped in as an ordinary member of the public bent on a spree instead of all this disguising her as somebody else—this Mrs. Amos B. whatever?"

"Too much of a risk. The lads on the desk at these casinos check and double-check everybody who comes in—passports, the lot. And they remember. The real Mrs. Herrington-Casey is a well-known gambler abroad but rarely comes to England. Miss Seeton, give or take a wig, a few pounds of makeup, a hundred pounds' worth or so of clothes and a few thousand pounds' worth of diamonds, is practically a dead ringer for her. We approached Mrs. H.-C. in France, where she is at the moment, on patriotic grounds—as the English widow of an American diplomat—and the cleaning up of gambling in general.

"They've been having the same sort of trouble over there

with a syndicate taking over the clubs and casinos, Mafia-style, so she was willing to play ball, lent us her passport and agreed to go to ground for a day or two. She's a game old girl, about ninety in the shade, and in full rig looks like a jeweler's display on feet."

Delphick grimaced. The idea of dolling up the unassuming little ex-children's drawing mistress as a jeweler's display struck him as the height of cruelty. Apart from that, "Syndicate," he said slowly. "We've had the odd beating-up here in Crime, and twice a killing, in which a syndicate's been mentioned. So far we've got nowhere on them—just talk about a syndicate, and the rumor it's run Mafia-style, but nothing concrete. We've drawn a blank as to what it is or who they are. Have you got any more?"

"We think so. No proof, mind you. We've pinpointed five men we think are running it—there may be more but I doubt it—and we think—again it's only think—that only the top man matters and if we can get him we'll break it. They're getting a hold on all gambling over here. They started on the race tracks; they've got a firm grip on the fun arcades; now they're taking over the casinos and moving in on the fairgound operators."

Delphick was surprised. "With regard to the casinos and clubs, can't the Gaming Board . . . ?"

"No, they can't—not without some sort of proof. All the clubs are licensed, so are all the employees, and everything looks on the up and up—was on the up and up till the syndicate moved in on 'em. The first sign was when the highfliers like The Gold Fish put up their stake limit from twenty-five to fifty quid. We can't prove they've been taken over and with no proof the Gaming Board can't act without a complaint—nor can we without a squeal."

"And no complaints?"

"No complaints," agreed Borden, "because of the muggings and killings you spoke of."

"But if the clubs got together . . ."

"They know damn well that by the time the law could move, more'n half of 'em'd be in hospital, or dead. Their 'getting together' is just what we're afraid of. Drive 'em far enough and they will—they'll get together and fight. We've got"—the inspector leaned forward and tapped the desk for emphasis—"to break the syndicate before it becomes an all-out war—with us caught in the crossfire. It's taken us nearly a year to get the picture. It's quite simple, really. An agent approaches the owners of the casinos and suggests a deal. He'll supply call girls and drugs for a percentage of the club's profits, guaranteeing that the increase in profits will leave the owner better off than before. If they don't increase, the syndicate takes nothing. Before the syndicate boys move in, they check the books to find out the average weekly profit. After that they put in a chartered accountant of their own to see the profits do go up."

"And if the proprietor turns the offer down?" asked Delphick.

"Kaput. A few muggings, the odd killing, but above all exit the casino in flames—a time bomb usually set to between four and five in the morning, when everyone's gone home. Eight clubs have gone that way so far this year, three of them in the last two months. What we can't get"— Borden thrust himself back in his chair, hands spread in frustration—"is an actual picture of the man at the top. Granted we've a pretty good idea who he is, but you can't get an ident on an idea—or circulate it. We've a few chummies lined up who might grass once we show we're closing in, but without a photograph we're stuck. Our man's a shy bird and every time we've tried for a mug shot we've failed. So our next best bet's a drawing—which brings us back to MissEss."

Delphick was worried. It was he who had been largely responsible for Miss Seeton's becoming attached to Scotland Yard on a retainer as an artist and in consequence he also felt responsible for her welfare. Her propensity for getting into trouble beyond the call of any duty—or rather drawing—she was required to do had him frequently on tenterhooks. So far her guardian angel, working overtime, had always intervened, but he felt that even the best-intentioned angel might get tired or get caught on the hop, and what would happen then? Restless, he got to his feet and crossed to the window.

"Was all this your idea or Commander Conway's?"

"Mine, actually, but the boss approved."

Without turning, Delphick hunched his shoulders. "You talk of a war—yet you're prepared to put Miss Seeton in the front line."

"We haven't," protested Borden. "She's only gone to The Gold Fish to observe—oh, all right," he conceded to the chief superintendent's unresponsive back, "as a scout, if you like, and with the best cover we could give her—"

"You're sure," interrupted Delphick, "that this top man of yours'll be at The Gold Fish tonight?"

"Pretty sure. He keeps a close eye on his investments and does the rounds. He'll turn up there sometime during the evening. Then Haley'll tip her the wink to memorize his mug and she'll lay it on the line for us tomorrow." Impatiently Delphick swung away from the window. "After all," Borden pointed out, "we've done our damnedest, and we had the devil of a job getting the expenses okayed. Apart from her clothes, the insurance on the jewelry alone'd give me and the missis and the kids a month's holiday in Spain. We didn't like to risk phony ice; we had to hire the real McCoy."

The chief superintendent returned to his desk and sat down heavily.

"Look, Oracle," Borden said, trying to lighten the mood. "Quit worrying about MissEss. Nothing'll happen. And Haley's there to look after her. From what he's seen and heard of her, he thinks she's the cat's mustache—that's why we put him in charge of her—and that as a detective she's a direct descendant of Nero Wolfe through Sherlock Holmes."

"Detective!" exploded Delphick. "She couldn't detect a sausage in its skin. If she saw a mugging in the street she'd deplore the violence but would be sure that if all the facts were known there'd probably be much to say on both sides. In fact, the first time we came up against her that's exactly what she did. A chummy was knifing his girl in the street.

What she saw was a gentleman hitting a lady and so she poked him in the back with her umbrella, all prepared to lecture him on manners. She was lucky to come out of that one alive." She'd been lucky, he reflected, to have come out of several subsequent episodes alive. How long would her luck last? "Does the A.C. know of this caper?"

"Sir Hubert? Sure. It had to be okayed by him and the receiver. And it was the A.C. who told us to—" The inspector laughed. "Well, knowing him, of course, he didn't tell us, he just thought that in the circumstances, or rather perhaps he should say in view of any possible circumstances that might arise he suggested that it might be wise to—i.e., he told us to fill you in. So I grabbed an early dinner and popped up to catch you soon as I heard you were back."

"I—" The chief superintendent broke off and rose quickly.

Sergeant Ranger stopped typing and sprang to his feet, cascading reports in triplicate to the floor. Inspector Borden looked round in surprise and jumped up.

"Oh—er—good evening, sir."

Sir Hubert Everleigh, Assistant Commissioner (Crime), resplendent in full evening dress, waved them to their seats.

"Please, gentlemen, don't let me disturb you. I only came in, rather perhaps I should say I dropped in, on my way to an embassy reception."

"I was just going, sir," said Borden hurriedly. "I'd just finished briefing the Ora—the chief superintendent on the MissEss—the Miss Seeton business." Sir Hubert smiled and nodded and the inspector made a thankful escape.

The assistant commissioner took the vacated chair. "Sit down, Chief Superintendent, and you"—he addressed the sergeant—"carry on with your paper chase. I don't want to delay you unduly; you must both be tired." Red of face and with a muttered "Thank you sir," the huge young sergeant scrabbled on the floor to retrieve his report. "I understand," said Sir Hubert, "that the business in Middlesborough ended satisfactorily."

The A.C., Delphick reflected, kept a firm finger on his department's pulse. "You've heard already, sir?"

"Oh, yes. The chief constable got in touch with me. He sounded very pleased and I gather that a man has been charged. I also gather that you have now been brought up to date with regard to events here, or to be more accurate, put in the picture regarding Miss Seeton's latest employment."

"Yes, sir."

"And"—he eyed Delphick quizzically—"you're not happy about it."

"No, sir."

"Quite. I didn't imagine that you would be, or not entirely. That was why I felt that you should be kept informed. On the face of it, the request from Fraud seemed reasonable, *is* reasonable, if a little expensive, but then you and I, particularly you, have a somewhat wider experience than they have of her proclivity for becoming unintentionally more deeply involved in—one might almost say of inadvertently becoming the crux of—any case to which she is assigned."

Delphick chewed his lip. "It's not so much what might happen in the casino, but for her to leave there covered in diamonds with only a detective constable could be asking for trouble. Would you object, sir, to my going over to The Gold Fish—not go in; just remain outside—and make sure she gets safely away?"

"Object?" Sir Hubert stood up. "No, I wouldn't object. There is no possible reason to suppose that anything untoward will occur, but experience has taught me that Miss Seeton and the untoward go hand in hand. If you would feel happier—and I'm bound to confess that I would share your emotion—to keep a fatherly eye on tonight's outcome, then in spite of the imposition in working overtime I would say go ahead." Having achieved his aim without having to make a definite request, Sir Hubert collected his gloves and went to the door. "I must be on my way or I shall be late, the ambassador will take offense and we shall have an international incident on our hands." At the door he paused. "That poor woman. Fraud have undoubtedly acted according to their best lights, but to overdress and overjewel her as they have smacks to me of the 1920s and E. Phillips Oppenheim, forgetting that Mr. Oppenheim said that in gambling establishments the world over, people are judged not by what they put upon themselves but by what they put upon the table." He shook his head. "Poor Miss Seeton. I cannot but feel that it may prove to be a disconcerting and embarrassing evening."

chapter

~2~

REALLY, CONSIDERED MISS Seeton, such a—such a disconcerting and embarrassing evening.

One had, of course, to do what one was told, but all this
dressing up, this disguise, seemed, somehow, so extreme.
The wig—a most improbable shade of mauve—was rather
hot and though, thank goodness, one could not see it
oneself, one was still conscious of the heavy makeup which
made one's face feel as if it were enameled and might crack.
And the false eyelashes with all that eyeblack on them were
stiff and heavy. The dress—so very shiny—had, one must
admit, a most becoming full-length skirt, but—she looked
down and looked hastily away—the bodice did start so very
late. And then the diamonds. Such a responsibility. Naturally people who could afford them wore them, but did they
really, she wondered, wear quite so many all at once?

Miss Seeton stifled a sigh. It would not, she felt, be in
keeping for this Mrs. Herrington-Casey to appear tired or
bored with her surroundings. Though she was. Or had been.
She'd had no idea that people who gambled took it so

seriously, with no laughter, no excitement; indeed, the
whole place struck her as a tinsel factory with joyless
workers performing a mechanical routine. Had been bored,
that was to say, until the arrival at the table of this girl. Who
was frightened. And that, in itself, seemed odd in a place
like this. And unaccompanied. That, too, struck her as
being strange. One knew, of course, that nowadays girls
could, and did, go where they liked alone. But though they
could, they didn't. Go, that was, to places such as this.
Unless, of course, they were girls of a certain type. Which
this girl palpably was not. Yet she was. Here alone, one
meant. And afraid. Miss Seeton had had too long an
experience of teaching children not to recognize fear
beneath apparent sophistication and a brash manner.

She put down her knife and fork. The food was very
good, if a little rich, and one would so have liked a glass of
water. She sipped her ginger beer. Quite pleasant, but so
gassy. It was very thoughtful of young Mr. Haley—no, she
must remember to call, to think of him as Tom—to make it
appear that she was drinking champagne, though she rather
feared that the champagne mixed with gin that he was
forced to drink was beginning to have something of an
effect.

Tom Haley pushed back his chair. "Come on, Mrs. H.-C.
Time to take 'em for a ride again." Dutifully Miss Seeton
rose. Haley got to his feet and stood blinking. He shook his
head; jolly hot in here. "You, too," he addressed the girl.
"Come 'n' join the gravy train. Rook 'em while the
rooking's good." A thought made him smile. After all the
kickup about the expenses for this jaunt, at the rate MissEss
was going, looked like the Yard'd be in clover. He only
hoped that once they'd taken their whack they'd let her keep
the rest as bonus. He negotiated the steps with care and
followed the two women down to the tables, where
gamblers' luck awaited them. The same seat at the same
table at which Miss Seeton had previously won was vacant.

Miss Seeton had tried. When, despite her protests that
she, of all people, should be sent to a casino, of all places,
to gamble, of all things, Miss Seeton *had* been sent, she had

felt it incumbent upon her to assimilate, so far as she was able, the rules of roulette and its idiom. She had therefore repaired to the public library in Brettenden to collect such literature as they had about the subject. Unfortunately, interesting as it was, naturally, to learn that the ancient Greeks spun shields and Romans chariot wheels and that considerably later Cardinal Mazarin had encouraged a game called *loca*—such a very odd word—which was apparently the first time that a ball had been used in conjunction with a spinning wheel, the rules and the idiom proved to be beyond her. And so very French. To begin with: the word *pair* presumably meant what it said; then *impair*, which must, she supposed, be the French for umpire; but *douzaine*, *carrée*, *en plein*, *colonne*, *manque*, *double*—yes, but double what?—*transversal pleine* and *à cheval* . . . She *had* tried, but finally she had had to admit defeat.

Tentatively Miss Seeton opened her handbag and selected a blue chip marked *25p*.

That last term—*à cheval*, or "to horse"—must refer in some way to the umpires, or croupiers as they were now called, since the word *croupier* meant someone who rode tandem on the rump of a horse. She looked forward toward the head of the table. The idea of one of those three elegant young men jogging on the hindquarters of a horse like some medieval Daisy Bell made her smile.

The smile died when from behind her chair Haley reached over, took the counter from her, selected five yellow chips marked £10 and placed them in her hand. Miss Seeton repressed a gasp: even her mathematics were equal to this addition. Fifty pounds? It seemed wickedly extravagant. However, she had not the right to argue and consoled herself with the thought that the sum was only a part of what she had already won. Admittedly, the first time, when Mr.—when Tom had staked to show her what to do, he had lost. But both times that she had played herself, they had given her back so many more of these sort of large tiddly-wink counters than she had put down. Though now that the girl's relief at winning had brought it home to her that these different-colored counters represented actual money, it all seemed—well, almost dishonest. Without looking, she obediently pushed the pile of yellow *jetons* onto the table.

The girl hesitated. Thirteen? The unlucky number? And black again? Dared she? A feeling of recklessness gripped her. Was it despair, champagne on an empty stomach, or something about this strange couple? The old woman was so serene, so casual, so—so certain somehow. Quickly, before she could change her mind, she followed the lead. She put down all her chips: the three yellow she had won directly on 13, using the blue *25p*'s, the pink *50p*'s, the black *£1*'s and her one white £5 to cover it on black, on odd, on low and on the dozen.

To an observer gamblers may appear impassive, but in actuality the habitual gamester is sensitive to the feeling of the "room." Miss Seeton's two previous flings had not gone unremarked and this, her third attempt, aroused a certain interest. When, after selecting the minimum with evident indifference, she smiled, changed her mind and placed the maximum stake on a single number, people began to gather round and even the woman in the raincoat and squashed felt hat left another table to stand and watch, with notebook at the ready.

Tom Haley took a deep breath. If old Borden ever found out, he'd get the sack; but what the hell—in for a penny, in for a thousand pounds. He dived into Miss Seeton's handbag, came up with a fistful of counters, selected the maximum and stacked his pile beside the other two on 13. To match the girl's plunge he sprinkled the rest of the handful around the table to back the bet all ways.

There was a movement among the onlookers. Some thrust forward impulsively to add their bets, then checked. Thirteen? Unlucky? Lucky? Three fliers already on it? Three, the charmed number. To add to it might upset the balance and negate one of the innumerable laws that governed their countless superstitions. While they wavered, the time for staking passed.

The croupier had spun the wheel. *"Rien ne va plus."*

Miss Seeton got up. She was right: Tom had had too much champagne. And too much gin. She made her way back to the supper table. If he was determined to throw away the police money—well, one supposed it was the public's money—then she would prefer not to watch. The attention of the spectators vacillated between concentration on the wheel and wonder at the bejeweled old woman who was so indifferent—so assured?—that she didn't bother to await the outcome.

Haley was dismayed. Miss Seeton's departure brought him momentarily to earth and his confidence evaporated. The wheel was slowing and the ball, too, seemed to lose confidence: it settled in one slot; flicked out and lodged in another; landed on a red and stayed there for one whole revolution before jumping up and starting on another round. He'd be back on the beat for sure—or traffic duty in a cul-de-sac. He closed his eyes and tried to remember prayers. By his side the girl stared relentlessly but saw nothing, knew nothing, except that she felt sick.

A murmur from the crowd aroused them. The wheel was still, the croupier's rake already functioning as it swept the counters up the table to his side. The ball was lying in—was lying in—oh, God, it wasn't true. The ball was lying in 13.

"Deirdre, my dear."

Color left the girl's face and the animation induced by her second win died. Her left hand, hovering over a cheese canapé, went rigid and her right, in putting down her champagne glass, slopped wine on the tablecloth.

So he'd been right. . . . Tom Haley was summoned from happy thoughts. He'd been told to see MissEss made a bit of a splash. Well, she had; taken the casino for a ride; pitched them into the water jump to the tune of over four thousand quid and they were still drying themselves off. But nobody'd told him to have a go too. Better ashk Mish—he pulled himself together—better tell her to keep mum about that. He realized he was in danger of getting squiffed. But just the same he'd still been right.

Although by now Haley's brain might be a little befuddled, his training stood him in good stead. While watching the girl at the bar, he had mentally filmed the sequence.

Running the film through his mind in slow motion had got him nowhere; normal tempo had not helped; but projecting it at double speed had given him an answer. The incessant movement of her hands, toying with her cigarette, her glass, pushing back or stroking her hair, the activity of her fingers in conversation with the barman, became clarified as a state of nervous tension. This girl was nervous—frightened. And from her present reaction, the man who'd just spoken to her was a possible cause. He looked at the man and trod on Miss Seeton's foot.

Oh. This, of course, was the signal that they had arranged. Miss Seeton glanced at her escort and realized that he was staring at the newcomer. This, then, must be the man whose features she must memorize. Handsome, if you cared for those sort of looks, she supposed. And he'd called the girl Deirdre. Such a pretty name. And suitable. Celtic in origin, she believed, and, if she remembered rightly, meant "the raging one." Which, again, had a certain suitability since, although she was convinced that the girl was scared, one could sense an underlying anger. For her own part, she did not. Care for his looks, she meant. Predatory, like a—like a hawk about to swoop. Or—was it too fanciful?—to judge by the pressure of his fingers on the girl's shoulder, a hawk that had already pounced.

"What a pleasant surprise," continued the new arrival. "I didn't know you played."

The girl shrugged off his hand. "I thought it was time I learned."

He laughed. "In the hope that the whirligig of time will bring in his revenges? You must be careful, my dear. Your mother's been having a worrying time, first with young Derrick making a fool of himself and then your father's accident. I was sorry to read about that, but luckily not too serious, from what the papers said. Please remember me to him. So don't try planning for too high stakes. We can't"—his tone had become openly taunting—"allow you to run wild; and don't forget troubles are apt to come in threes." He switched to social polish. "But that's enough of trouble. Won't you introduce me to your friends?"

With evident reluctance she replied, "Mrs. Herrington-

Casey, may I have the pleasure"—she flicked the word with
sarcasm—"to present Mr. Thatcher. Mr. Thatcher—Mr.
Haley."

Thatcher bowed to Miss Seeton. "We are honored, Mrs.
Herrington-Casey. You rarely play in England, I understand. You won't recollect"—his eyes mocked her—"but
we met once, only a brief introduction, at—Monte?" He
fingered his lower lip. "Or was it Cannes?" He smiled.
"But there, I mustn't interrupt. You appear to be winning
at the moment and"—he bowed again and his smile
broadened—"I might spoil your game."

That had torn it. Haley watched Thatcher move across to
the bar. Why the hell hadn't Research done their homework
properly? From the photographs he'd seen of Mrs. Herrington-Casey, MissEss looked near enough, but if Thatcher had
actually met her . . . Well, could be she'd got by, but not
to trush—not to rely on it. Unpleasant type. Everything
he'd said could've had a double meaning. "You won't
recollect . . ." "You 'pear to be winning at the moment . . ." "I might shpoil your game." Better take it
he'd rumbled her. Hell—they'd better make tracks.

Light began to filter through the alcoholic mist. Got
it. Deirdre. Thought he knew the face. In all the glosh—in
the magazhines. Mos' beautiful face he'd ever—mos'
beau'ful . . . The girl became restive under his glassy
stare and Haley tried to round up his scattering wits. 'At
was right—ol' Lord Kenharding's daughter. An' his lordship'd smashed up his car last week. There'd been a photo
of the whole fam'ly—'at was right, Derrick, teen-age son
an' heir, and the press'd rehashed about the silly young oaf
being copped at some drug shindig and'd got off with a fine
and a wigging. Come to that, bad form Thatcher bringing
up all that family stuff in front of strangers. Or was it? Had
all that been double-talk too?

Haley's thought stumbled along their backward track.
What'd he said to her? " 'Member me to him," over the ol'
man's accident. "Don't try playing for too high stakes"—
nothing in that unless the Honorable Deirdre was up to
something; "can't allow you to run wild" and "troubles are

apt to come in threes.'' Hm, could be innoc—could be all right, but could jus' as well be a threat. From Thatcher's manner and from what he knew of the bastard, could damn well be a threat.

How very awkward. Miss Seeton regarded Thatcher's back. If he had met this Mrs. Herrington-Casey, however briefly, he must have known. Surely? She looked at Tom Haley for guidance, but he appeared to be immersed. In thought. What an unpleasant man. Mr. Thatcher, she meant. Not that one had any reason to think so—he'd been perfectly polite—but such a sardonic, almost a sneering, manner. Perhaps one's view was colored by knowing what one did. Or rather not knowing what one didn't. But she did know that the police were interested in him and that generally meant that there was something unsatisfactory and that might easily have influenced one's opinion. As for the girl, her mouth was set and she had gone very pale. But more with temper now, one thought, than with fear. Certainly it had been regrettable manners for Mr. Thatcher to mention her family's affairs in front of strangers, though possibly he did not realize that they were—strangers, that was—and certainly one could not take exception to his commiserating over the father's accident; again it had only been his manner. But Derrick—persumably her brother— having made a fool of himself: whatever he had done, to speak of it in front of other people was embarrassing and in deplorable taste.

Abruptly Deirdre Kenharding stood up. "Thank you for the champagne and everything. Sorry if I was rude." She was gone before Haley, slow in reaction and struggling to his feet, could find words to prevent her.

"Got all you want, MissEss?" he murmured. "I mean seen enough of the Thatcher bloke to get him down on paper?" Miss Seeton nodded. "Good. Don't know if he cottoned to the Mrs. H.-C. lark, but think better shkip coffee 'nd get weaving."

It was an accurate description of his own movements as, having paid the bill, he followed his companion down the steps and weaved his way after her toward the desk by the main doors, where he changed her chips for money. A check was offered for so large an amount but he waved the suggestion aside and insisted on cash. Gosh. Never handled so much oof in his life—and wasn't likely to again. Over four thousand smackers. Boy. He crammed the majority into Miss Seeton's handbag until it would barely close, stuffed the rest into his pockets and ushered her into the foyer.

In an upstairs office, Thatcher was waiting for a report. The telephone shrilled and the casino's proprietor picked up the receiver.

"Yes?" He listened for a short while, made some notes, thanked the instrument, replaced it and turned to Thatcher. "There is a Thomas E. Haley, a detective constable attached to the Fraud Squad, and"—he glanced down at his notes— "the description fits."

"Right." Thatcher pulled at his lower lip. "Then I'll make an inspired guess who the old woman is. Some artist—I've forgotten her name—they use quite a bit. This'll be their answer to failing to get a photograph." He put his hands in his pockets and began to pace the room. "I'll put a stop to that. She's clever or been lucky or both, or the press find her good copy. It was luck, the Kenharding girl being with them, or they might have got away with it."

The proprietor's expression was sour. "I should've thought the luck was their trying to pass her off as someone you happened to know."

"I don't know her—I met her once." He frowned. "They'd done a good job. Anybody who'd only seen Herrington-Casey around casually would've been fooled by it. What I want to know is, is Deirdre in on it? They didn't come together; the barman told me the girl arrived alone. Keep tabs on all three. I want to know when they're leaving."

"Look, you're not going to start anything here. You've taken over and unfortunately I can't quarrel with that—"

"And your profits are up. You don't quarrel with that either."

"I don't. But apart from the men you've put in here—and

I prefer not to know the reason—you promised there'd be no trouble. I'm responsible to my directors for the running of the casino—"

"And one of your directors," cut in Thatcher smoothly, "Lord Kenharding, had a nasty accident the other day when his brakes failed on a hill near his home. He was lucky to get off with minor injuries, but somehow I don't think he'll be in a mood to quarrel with anybody for a while. Life is so uncertain these days. . . . His wife or daughter could have accidents too."

The proprietor thought over the implications. Then: "What d'you want me to do?"

"Nothing more than I've told you: keep tabs on Haley—I think he's been drinking—on the woman and on Deirdre. They're well up at the moment; if they cash their chips, how much for and whether they take it in cash or check; and a warning as soon as any of them show sings of going." He laughed at the proprietor's expression. "Don't worry. Nothing will happen in the casino—and for the rest, the less you know, the better."

Haley retrieved his coat and the mink stole which completed Miss Seeton's outfit. He grinned to himself; for once she hadn't been allowed to carry her umbrella. The papers had always played it up, calling her "The Battling Brolly," and it was known at the Yard as her "small arms." Oh, well—they were on their way with what they'd come for—and considering all that lolly, rather more than they'd bargained for—and even if Thatcher had wrinkled her there was damn all he could do about it now. . . . Pity the girl had sloped off; he'd like to've . . . Oh, well. Old Kenharding's daughter; out of his class. But still— Turning too quickly to hand Miss Seeton the stole, he crossed his legs, stumbled over his foot and nearly fell, thereby failing to observe Miss Seeton's difficulties.

Worried over her responsibility for such a large sum of money, she was keeping a firm grip on the ornamental clasp of her handbag, insecure now that it was overfull, and she was unprepared to receive the long length of the fur which

was suddenly thrust at her. This, too, was valuable. And it
wasn't hers. Now, how was it they'd shown her to wear it?
It was quite heavy, with those lead weights sewn into the
seams at both ends. If she put it across her shoulders it
might easily slip, trail on the floor and become damaged. To
drape it over her arms posed the same problem, and holding
it in place would mean that the bag, especially with that
very scratchy clasp, would rub the fur. There was some
simple way, if only she could remember. . . . Of course.
How stupid. One put it over one's shoulders and, leaving
the left side hanging down, you threw the right side over the
left shoulder and the weights balanced it and kept the
wretched thing in place. Miss Seeton executed the maneuver with a determined lack of skill: too little hung; too much
was flung.

The doorman, a recent employee, alerted by the desk
inside that two of the party he was to watch for were
leaving, was hurrying forward to open the main doors,
where, as a prearranged signal to the men waiting outside,
he was to blow his nose. He side-stepped to avoid Tom
Haley's gyrations. There was one what weren't in a fit state
to be driving. He smirked. Well, the boss was seeing to it
neither of 'em'd be in a fit state for a bit. The lead weight of
Miss Seeton's flying stole landed full in the man's eye and
he uttered a word that would have ensured instant dismissal
in most establishments. Temporarily blinded, hand pressed
to his streaming eyes, he lost the handicap race to the doors.
Haley pushed one of the glass panels open and tottered after
Miss Seeton to the head of the steps leading down the
pavement. The doorman, a bad third but trying to atone for
lost time, appeared behind them waving a handkerchief,
into which he trumpeted as though stricken by the first stage
of flu.

Even forewarned, Delphick was shocked when Miss
Seeton appeared at the top of the steps. Their car was
parked on the opposite side of the street, facing the casino,
and sensing his superior's quickened interest, Sergeant
Ranger leaned forward over the steering wheel to get a
better view.

"What, sir?"

"Use your eyes, Bob—just coming out."

Obediently, the sergeant's eyes opened wide. That—that Christmas tree, Aunt Em? It couldn't be. She . . . He grasped the door handle. "Do we . . . ?"

"No, we've no standing in this; we just—" He broke off when Miss Seeton's escort came into view. "Isn't that Haley?"

"Yes, sir."

"He's drunk."

Bob Ranger studied the swaying figure. "Yes, sir."

The doorman appeared, handkerchief flapping. A car across the road jerked into motion, stopped in front of the entrance. Two men sprang from it.

"Out," snapped Delphick. "Something's up."

The two men who had been awaiting the doorman's signal were confused. What the hell was Joe up to, rushing out like that, flippin' his wiper like a bleedin' tablecloth and then blowing into it like he was sounding the Last Post? Did he mean the old cow who'd just come out 'nd if so, why hadn't he warned 'em first like arranged? Trust Joe to make a muck of it. They realized that their quarry, now halfway down the steps, was liable to escape.

"You take 'er, Lofty," said the shorter of the two, "and bung 'er in the car. I'll see to 'is nibs—'e's pissed."

"C'mon." The taller man grabbed Miss Seeton's arm. "In the car quick or I'll do yer."

"I think," said Miss Seeton, drawing herself up so that she reached nearly to his shoulder, "that you must have made a mistake."

Tom Haley was in trouble. The night air had hit him like a blow, completing the work so well begun by gin and champagne. Below him rippled the flight of steps, expanding to grace a palace, contracting to one short pace from the pavement, which billowed at their base. He put out a cautious foot like a bather testing the temperature. A short man—short men?—rushed at him. Training reacted and he swerved, a movement which undid them both; to recover his balance, Haley performed a high kick that would have secured him a place in any chorus line, came down astride his adversary's neck, scissored the man's head in an attempt to keep his seat and rode his unwilling charger down into the back of Miss Seeton's assailant.

Lofty was first on his feet. Shorty had had it, by the looks. He saw Tom Haley sprawled on hands and knees, trying to rise. Easy. He let the cosh drop from his sleeve on its wrist thong, bent, and raised it above the exposed neck.

Miss Seeton realized his intent. "Stop that!" she commanded. What could she . . . ? She had nothing. . . . Instinctively she slapped the handbag against his head; the gilt bird's-claw clasp ripped his temple, he yowled, and the bag burst open, showering the combatants with some three thousand pounds' worth of confetti.

Lofty's right hand was caught in a viselike grip and wrenched behind his back in a hammer lock, while Delphick pulled Haley to his feet and held him to prevent his falling.

"Considering your state, which will need some explaining, that was nice work and quick thinking."

" 'Nksh," said Haley.

The giant Bob Ranger, still holding Miss Seeton's attacker, plucked Shorty off the ground by his collar, held him up, examined the gash on his forehead and remarked, "This one's a bit broken, sir, and'll need stitching. Doubt he'll come round for a while."

A uniformed officer approached the group. "Now, then, what . . . ?" He recognized Delphick. "Sorry, sir. I didn't know you were in charge. I've called in already and they're sending a patrol. Anything I can do?"

"I'm not in charge," explained the chief superintendent. "We—er—just happened to be here when it started. If you'll cuff that one"—he indicated Lofty—"and hold him till the car— Ah." He heard an approaching siren. "Here it comes. Good. Then if you'll help keep these people back"—passers-by were beginning to collect in an excited group—"perhaps we can pick up all this stuff." He pointed to the money and it began to dawn on him that the greater part of it was in twenty- and ten-pound notes. "What've you been up to—pinching the till?" He let go of Haley. "Get on with it."

Released, Tom Haley subsided happily. "Oodles o' lovely oof," he chortled. He put his hand in his coat pocket and produced another bundle; offered it to Delphick. "Have some. Got losh more."

Delphick ignored him. He observed that Bob Ranger, relieved of his first prisoner, was still holding Shorty by the collar. "Sergeant," he directed, "put that down before you strangle it. And if you've got a clean handkerchief," he added, "tie up its head till an ambulance comes." The sergeant obeyed and joined Delphick and Miss Seeton in retrieving the money. The chief superintendent smiled at her. "Would it be too much to ask what exactly has been going on?"

Immediately he regretted the word "exactly." Exactitude, particularly in regard to her relations with the police, was almost a vice with Miss Seeton. Her thoughts gamboled along their irresponsible way, and through backtracking in order to ensure that no point had been missed and that her meaning was clear, her explanations were frequently incomprehensible. Before she could answer, the police car arrived and by virtue of rank Delphick was forced to abandon the treasure hunt and give instructions for the removal and interrogation of one prisoner—to be charged pro tem with assaulting a police officer—for the hospitalization of Shorty, who was beginning to moan his way back to consciousness but was likely to prove a concussion case, and for holding back the crowd, which was growing larger. The handkerchief-waving doorman, he noted for future reference, had retired into the casino and taken no further part in the proceedings. He returned as Miss Seeton and Bob Ranger were collecting the last of the scattered notes.

"Well?" he asked her.

"I think," she replied, "that it was a mistake."

The understatement of the month. He forbore to laugh. "I'm inclined to agree with you, but on whose part and about what?"

"It was the taller man—the one you sent away with the policeman. He asked—well, actually he told me to get into the car. I said that I thought he must be making a mistake, but before he had time to answer, Mr. Haley and the other one—I didn't, of course, see exactly what happened since they were behind me—fell down beside us and he—the tall one, I mean—was going to hit Mr. Haley and as he didn't stop when I told him to, I did. Hit him, that is to say. On the head, and it burst. The handbag, I mean."

"Did he say anything else, beyond telling you to get in the car? Did he give any reason?"

"No. That's why I'm sure it was a mistake. You see, there was no reason."

He regarded her. Apart from the bulging bag, with all those diamonds she positively dripped reasons. Let it ride. Maybe they'd get something out of the two men. "What about the doorman?" he asked. "From what Bob and I could see, he appeared to be signaling—waving a handkerchief about and blowing his nose."

Miss Seeton flushed. "Oh, no. That, I'm afraid, was me."

"You?"

"Yes. I hit him in the eye. With a lead weight," she added. She had a feeling that perhaps she had not made herself quite clear. "I'm not used to fur stoles," she explained.

We're off again, thought Bob gloomily. Fraud had brought her into this, just for one evening, but that wouldn't be the end of it—not by a long chalk; not with Aunt Em. Once she started up, there was no stopping her. She'd be right there in the thick of things till the end of the case, with the rest of them running round in circles trying to pick up the pieces.

In a curious way Delphick felt cheered. He had become so accustomed to Miss Seeton and her umbrella, and to the way it appeared to go into action in her defense of its own volition, that he had come to look upon it as a talisman without which she might be vulnerable. Now it was evident that any inanimate object—fur stoles, handbags, the whole armory of a woman's paraphernalia—might well become lethal in her hands.

"What arrangements had they made for you to change and get home?" he asked.

"I don't know," she confessed. "Mr. Haley was seeing to everything and I—"

" 'S right," interrupted Haley, staggering to his feet. " 'M in charge. 'Ll take her—take her . . ." His voice trailed away. Take her where? Couldn't 'member—not at the moment. It'd come back. But not standing up. Standing up gave everything the shakes. Look at 'em all shaking. Lots of cars and lots of people—all shaking. He sat down again with a giggle. " 'Nd lots o' lolly," he confided to no one in particular.

Delphick hesitated. What was he to do with this young ass? He'd gone to Miss Seeton's rescue like a trooper, at risk of a broken arm or leg or neck, for that matter. If he took him back to the Yard in this state, the boy'd be for the high jump. And was he genuinely drunk, or had somebody slipped something into his drink?

"Where do you live?"

"Wash—what . . . ?" Haley bleared up at him. He blinked. "Gosh, Chief Shoop—Sup—" But "Superintendent" was beyond him. "It's the Oracle," he mumbled. He tried to rise but his legs betrayed him and he knelt before Delphick in an attitude of prayer.

Delphick bit his lip, but his shoulders shook. "Bob." For once he broke his rule never to address his subordinate except by rank in public. "Take this religious novice to the car, stick him in the front seat and let him sleep it off. Perhaps he'll make some sense when he comes to; I could bear to learn what's gone on. We're taking you home now," he told Miss Seeton. "I'll see you get your clothes back tomorrow."

"But, Chief Superintendent," she protested, "it's much too far. I can easily take a train."

"Not in that rig, you can't," retorted Delphick. "Your

last train's probably gone and how do you imagine you'd get home from the station? Walk?"

"Oh, no. You see, I left my bicycle at the station this morning and it's only two miles."

A bicycle? This was a new development. The thought of Miss Seeton, in baubles, bangles and beads, breezing along a country lane in the dark was almost too much for him. "No argument. We're responsible for those gewgaws you're wearing, to say nothing of all the money you seem to have swiped—which I still want to hear about. You follow Bob over to the car and get in the back. I'll settle one or two things here and be with you in a few minutes. Did you come by car or taxi?"

"By taxi. Mr. Haley said it would be less—"

"Good. Off you go."

The crowd was beginning to scatter since the principal actors had left the stage, the ambulance had come and gone, only the police remained and no further amusement appeared to offer.

Delphick arranged for the registration of the raiders' car to be checked and the car to be removed and examined, although the fact that the driver had slipped away at some point during the fracas almost certainly meant that it had been stolen. They were unlikely to get any help there and must hope that the men they'd caught would sing. He sent a message to the Yard for Inspector Borden, explaining that he was taking Miss Seeton home to Kent, that Haley was with them, that he himself would be responsible for her borrowed plumes and would bring them back to London.

Should he question the doorman or not? Better perhaps for the look of the thing, though he was pretty sure he'd get nowhere. He was right. Joe Flackman insisted that he hadn't seen nothing nor heard nothing. The silly old cow'd flipped her bleedin' fur in 'is kisser and what with his eye watering and his nose running, he couldn't've told you if it was Friday night or Christmas, so he'd gone back in and let 'em get their own bleedin' taxi and bad cess to 'em and no tip neither, which you'd've thought, considering, was the least.

Delphick did not remedy the deficiency and returned to his car. Joe Flackman would keep: small fry, but he'd pass on the name to Borden, and it supported the inspector's contention that this syndicate was putting their own men into these places. The Gold Fish's reputation had been good, top of its class, but . . . Anyway, none of it was his pigeon, though he had an uneasy suspicion that now that Miss Seeton had entered the lists there was a definite possibility it might become so. His instinct in coming here tonight had been right and somehow he doubted it would end there. Meanwhile, to get her home. He grinned to himself at the thought of the village's reaction to the sight of her in her present finery—that would start the tongues wagging full tilt. He checked his watch; nearly ten. Luckily, Plummergen was only about six miles beyond Brettendon, which made it about seventy miles all told—yes, it would take them all of two hours. Good, the village should be safely bedded down and she could slip into her cottage without anybody being the wiser.

chapter

~3~

THE HARVEST DANCE at the Plummergen village hall was proving to be its annual success, even better attended than usual, and the jollification had been helped by an extension of the license at the George and Dragon until midnight. The revelers were pouring out onto the village's only street from both hall and hostelry for protracted good nights and discussion before dispersing to their homes.

A car coming slowly down the Street attracted attention. 'T'weren't local. Furriners, likely. But where'd they be goin' this time o' night? Someone recognized Bob Ranger at the wheel. Ah, t'one what'd married Dr. Knight's darter. Well, 'e were goin' t'wrong way, then. 'E'd likely be callin' on that Miss Seeton. What—late as this? Any road she weren't there; gone gallivantin' off t'morning to Lunnon and weren't back yet, as anybody with gumption knew cos 'er bike were still out at t'station.

Instead of carrying on through the village, where the Street narrowed suddenly between the wall that bounded Miss Seeton's garden and the next house before widening again to become the main road to the coast, the car veered right toward Marsh Road, the only other exit at the south end of Plummergen, swung round in a circle and drew up before Miss Seeton's cottage. This maneuver placed it in an ideal position for the villagers. The car now faced the George and Dragon, set back on the opposite side of the Street, so that the group in front of the inn and the crowd emerging from the village hall had an uninterrupted view of the proceedings. They all edged forward, apparently engrossed in conversation but waiting agog for this next episode in Miss Seeton's saga. They were well rewarded. From the car stepped an elderly lady, bedizened, bediamonded, befurred and with coils of improbable mauve-white hair. A tall man with graying hair followed her. 'Twere that Lunnon tec what were 'ere afore, stayin' at t' George with 'is sargint. Interest quickened. That Miss Seeton were in trouble agin. Done summit in Lunnon 'nd they'd found 'er out 'nd down here to search 'er house, 'im 'nd sargint. But what for they'd brought t' beaded old bag with 'em? Bob Ranger joined Delphick and helped him to extract Haley, while Miss Seeton, smiling and nodding to one or two people whom she knew, went ahead of them up the short path to Sweetbriars. The smiles and nods took effect.

" 'Tis 'er."

" 'Tain't."

" 'Tis, I say. 'S 'erself, an' in disguise."

At the door, as she searched for her key, a few notes fluttered from Miss Seeton's bag; quickly she stooped to recover them. The buzz went round.

"See them notes?"

"T' bag's stuffed with 'em."

"Robbed a bank likely 'nd down 'ere to share 't out quietlike."

"Allus said pleece weren't no better'n t' next."

Moral indignation, since the watchers were not being asked to share the proceeds, began to soar and was given voice by two ladies in the posse from the hall, one short and plump, the other tall and thin, who were watching avidly, since here indeed was material for the gossip upon which they thrived.

"This—it's too much," fluted the well-rounded Mrs. Blaine. "It's too dreadful. How dare she come here dressed like that. It's too—"

"Disgusting," supplied the angular Miss Nuttel.

"And look." Mrs. Blaine clutched her companion's arm. "Just look at that. It's too—it's too—"

For the first time in many years words failed them both as Delphick and Bob assisted the hapless Haley, half asleep and virtually legless, into the cottage.

"Poor lad, he's ill," exclaimed a motherly soul.

"Bain't," contradicted an elderly farm laborer, whose complexion lent the color of authority to his statement. " 'E's pissed."

"Wounded mebbe."

"Pissed," repeated veteran authority.

"Knifed, I reckon."

"Drugged, I'd say."

"Nar," said authority. "Like what I told yer—pissed."

And upon relished argument and speculation the door to Sweetbriars closed.

The bar in the George and Dragon was crowded at lunchtime the next day and Miss Seeton *in absentia* held the floor. Her detractors and supporters argued hotly, although the latter were in the invidious position of having no firm foundation for debate. Unsuitably attired she had undoubtedly been; drunk, or possibly wounded, one of her companions had been; under police escort she had been and too much money she had had. These were facts and even her most fervent admirers could produce no convincing explanation, whereas the opposition, unbounded by probability, interpreted at their pleasure.

The news of the disturbance outside The Gold Fish had made a short paragraph and heading in the morning papers, but beyond Miss Seeton's name—the police were uncertain how this had been leaked—and an admission that two men had been detained, one of them in hospital, there was little to go on. The local press were present, listening and questioning, since their attempts to interview the heroine herself had been thwarted by Miss Seeton's daily help.

In the crowd were two people who spoke little but absorbed the atmosphere and the discussion.

Mel Forby from the *Daily Negative* had been to Plummergen before and had worked her way onto the inside track of one of Miss Seeton's earlier escapades. Originally a fashion reporter, noted for a tough manner, an acid tongue and a spurious mid-Atlantic accent, she now had a weekly page and also wrote the stories and "balloons" for a comic strip about village life based broadly on Miss Seeton herself and Plummergen. Influenced by the ex-art teacher's admiration for the interesting bone structure of her face and her beautiful eyes, Mel had abandoned the excessive eye makeup and dropped her aggressive manner, and the accent, too, had fallen by the way.

Thrudd Banner was a free-lance foreign correspondent. He had met Miss Seeton in Switzerland, followed her, and the story, to Paris, but had missed the final episode at customs on her return to England. He had never been able to make up his mind whether Miss Seeton was the innocent victim of circumstances or the greatest liar he had ever met. Believing in her, trying to help and to protect her until events or her own actions appeared to prove him wrong, he had frequently ended by kicking himself for a gullible fool. In Switzerland such an event had led him, for the first time in his life, to fire a pistol—and miss—in her defense. Miss Seeton's gun, going off by accident, had also missed, but since her opponent had stumbled and fallen to his death, to Thrudd she had appeared the perfect markswoman. Now home on holiday, he had scented copy in the report of the previous night's affair and was once more on her trail. He noticed the woman at the bar, straightened, squared his shoulders, looked again, his eyes widening.

"Mel Forby, by God."

Mel turned slowly. "My mother made no such claim." She smiled disarmingly. "Why, Thrudd. Home? What has England done to deserve such dishonor? Has the Continent become too hot to hold you?"

Thrudd was momentarily thrown off balance by the change in looks, manner and accent; then he rallied. "No, Mel. I came simply to give you the benefit of my experience and to guide your faltering footsteps along the path of true communication with your public—both of them—and I'll even, on request, correct your spelling."

Mel's eyebrows lifted, she picked up her drink and continued her conversation with a Kent reporter. Thrudd addressed her back:

"I'm the first to admit that women have their place in journalism and the last to deny they don't know it." Getting no reply, he taunted: "The simplest answer to the unanswered is no answer, and to retire from battle is to live to fight a lesser opponent on another day." He raised his voice. "My dear Lady Disdain, are you yet listening?" Still he failed to get a rise. "A waste of ammunition," he mused aloud. "But then you could hardly expect the Bard to be appreciated on the women's page."

Mel looked round in gentle feigned surprise. "I wonder that you will still be talking, Signior Bannerdick, nobody marks you."

Thrudd laughed. "For that I'll buy you a drink and as we're obviously here for the same purpose I might—just might—introduce you to MissEss."

"I'll have a whisky and for that I might not—just might not—warn Miss S. against you."

"You know her?"

"Mm."

"Then let us repair to a corner table, down weapons and plan campaign."

Martha Bloomer slammed the front door of Sweetbriars and went into the sitting room. Martha saw herself, with some justification, in the privileged position of a family retainer, having "done for" the previous incumbent of Sweetbriars, old Mrs. Bannet, until she died, and was now "doing for" her goddaughter and devisee, Miss Seeton.

"There," she announced. "Let's hope that's the last of 'em—nosey lot of Parkers. Not but what you don't ask for it the way you carry on whisking off to London and gambling and coming back dressed like that you can't expect but what people'll notice and want to know—"

"I told you, Martha—" Miss Seeton had told her several times, but Martha was not to be diverted.

"Yes I know and I've nothing against the police not in the ordinary way though the way they went on about Stan's bike lamp when all that was wrong was the battery was run down and if it makes things easier for you being able to afford washing-up machines and bikes and the like then I've got nothing to say but I must say they ought to be more careful and you too or one day we'll have you getting yourself killed and then where'll you be I'd like to know."

Miss Seeton had no wish to speculate upon her future state and was tired of the argument. "It was just very unfortunate that it was the night of the Harvest Dance, otherwise no one would have known about it. In any case, they'll soon forget. It's over and finished. The police only wanted a drawing of a gentleman's face. The chief superintendent wouldn't let me do it last night. He said we were all tired and we needed coffee—black, of course, for Mr. Haley. So I must start on it soon because someone's coming down to fetch it." She glanced at the clock. "Oughtn't you to be at home, Martha? What about Stan's lunch?"

"I left Stan a cold dinner and told him I'd not be back till tea and he's fetching your bike from the station on his way home and he'll bring it after his tea when he comes over to cut the grass. I'm not leaving you on your own with people popping in all the time and no one at the door to tell them no." Having outtalked opposition, Martha became indulgent. "I've made you a nice mince and veg so your dinner's ready and you can have it in here with Welsh rabbit for afters."

Her lunch disposed of, Miss Seeton settled to work. The hawklike face, so clear in her memory, refused to appear as a conventional portrait on paper. She tore up several attempts and sat, thoughtful. Her hand began to stray: lines, free-running and vital, became a bird on a cliff edge with

one leg raised. From its claw fell flaming buildings
disintegrating in the air and out of the buildings tumbled
people. Under the bird's other talons were four figures,
crushed to the rock, two male, two female; three of them lay
flat, spread-eagled, but one woman, caught only by the
heel, was struggling to get free. The raised face, in
miniature, bore a resemblance to Deirdre Kenharding.
Behind the bird a nest showed eggs, from one of which a
beak was beginning to emerge.

Sadly Miss Seeton contemplated the cartoon. So very
fanciful. And, of course, no use. The bird was, she was
prepared to admit, a good likeness of Mr. Thatcher. But
hardly what was wanted. She could not bring herself to
destroy the sketch, so she put it to one side and tried again.
Finally she produced a painstaking portrait of Thatcher: it
was worthy, it was detailed, it was lifeless. There. That, she
felt, would do. It was the sort of thing they needed. With
relief she put away her drawing materials, slipped the
cartoon into a portfolio and stowed it in a drawer of her
writing desk. The portrait she enclosed in a large envelope
to await the arrival of whoever was sent to fetch it.

A knock at the front door heralded another visitor. She
half rose from her seat, then remembered that Martha was
staying on today and dealing with intruders.

Martha appeared in the doorway. "It's a young lady won't
give her name—says you wouldn't know it—but says you
know her. I told her no but she wouldn't have it, says it's
very important and she must see you."

Deirdre Kenharding pushed past her into the room.
"Please, Miss Seeton, I didn't know who you were last
night, but it is important, really. I must talk to you—
please." Gone was the arrogance of assumed sophistication:
a very pretty girl, beautiful when she smiled, in trouble and
appealing.

"It's all right, Martha," said Miss Seeton, and turned to
her guest. "Have you had lunch—would you like some
coffee?"

"No, nothing, thanks. It's just about last night. I must
talk to you."

"Please sit down. I—" She broke off as another knock sounded. They heard an argument, then Martha returned.

"A lady and gentleman says you know them which you do her seeing it's that Miss Forby from the paper that was here before and he says he knew you abroad which don't seem likely because he don't sound it, more like English to me, but is sure you'll want to see them."

"Of course she does, don't you, Miss S.?" Mel breezed in, followed by Thrudd Banner. "This dragon of yours"— she grinned at Martha—"was determined—" She stopped on seeing the girl. "Oh, sorry. We didn't know you'd got somebody with you." And the Honorable Deirdre at that, reflected Mel. Miss S. certainly got around. "Now"—she bent and kissed Miss Seeton lightly on the cheek— "what've you been getting up to this time? It's good to see you—and too long, but you live so far away." She felt the constraint and sought to lighten the atmosphere. "May I go and rustle up some coffee? The stuff at the George is revolting, and I remember my way round the kitchen."

"I'll get it," said Martha, and departed.

Miss Seeton had risen. Oh, dear. This was all really rather awkward. If only . . . And then again, she wasn't sure how to introduce them. One should, of course, present the younger to the elder, except for the men, and that, naturally, was the other way about. Because of sex. Being different, she meant. But she didn't know the girl's surname and to call her Deirdre on such slight acquaintance would be most incorrect. Certainly she couldn't do that. "Deirdre," said Miss Seeton, "may I present Miss Forby and Mr. Banner."

They all found seats and there was an uneasy silence. To break the ice Thrudd asked Miss Seeton chattily:

"Been doing much shooting lately?"

It broke nothing but the silence. Mel and Thrudd tried together.

"Miss S. . . ."

"MissEss . . ."

Both stopped. "You know," observed Thrudd, "the way you pronounce that, I'd say you spelled it differently."

"You know," retorted Mel, "the way you pronounce that, I'd say you're copying a mistake by the Yard's computer. Mine's original, yours is duplicated."

The conversation sank for the third time and the noise of a car drawing up outside and yet one more knock upon the door was almost welcome.

"Mr. Delphick," announced Martha.

Miss Seeton rose with relief, Mel's and Thrudd's identical beams expressed "We've hit pay dirt," while Deirdre Kenharding shrank back in her armchair. Deirdre was beginning to realize that she had been a fool. From the morning papers she had concluded that it must have been Miss Seeton whom she had met the night before. Impulsively she had decided to go and see her with an appeal for help. Her own effort to extract information from the barman at the casino had been a failure and, when she was unable to think of what next she could do, the encounter with the older woman had appeared to be a pointer from Fate which must not be ignored. The *Daily Negative* had padded its report with a short summary of Miss Seeton's exploits, mentioning the name of the village where she lived. Having found Plummergen on the map, the girl had set off by car, eaten an early lunch on the way and on her arrival in the village had found it to be merely a question of asking for directions to Sweetbriars at the post office cum general store.

Reading that Miss Seeton was retained by Scotland Yard as an artist but was not an actual member of the police force, although the newspapers were inclined to make much of her powers as a detective, Deirdre felt that Miss Seeton might be able to help in a private capacity, keep confidence, yet still have authority behind her should it be needed. Intent upon her own problem, it had not occurred to her that after the trouble outside the casino the police would still be in evidence and that inevitably the press, too, would be upon the scene. Deirdre had walked straight into the very company she most wished to avoid. However, now that the damage was done, the only thing to do was to express a natural interest in Miss Seeton's welfare—although, as she ruefully admitted, a journey of seventy miles was an unnaturally long expression—and to try and outstay the visitors.

Delphick sensed the strain in the room. He had hoped to see Miss Seeton alone and for her to be entertaining was unusual. That she should appear out of her depth was nothing abnormal, but for Mel Forby not to be in command of any situation was; the other two he didn't know.

Martha brought in a tray. "I brought biscuits as well, seeing you're making a real party of it." She placed the tray on the coffee table by the fire, pulled up a chair for Delphick, looked at the other guests with disapproval, sniffed and left the room.

Since Miss Seeton appeared to be at a loss, Mel performed the introductions. Thrudd Delphick dismissed: more press—only to be expected; but Kenharding . . . So this was the girl Haley, when sobered up, had mentioned in his report. Her presence here today could hardly be pure chance—that would be stretching coincidence's arm a little far. He decided to go ahead as though the others weren't there; it could do no harm at this juncture and might stir something up. He smiled encouragingly at his hostess.

"Done your homework?"

"Why, yes, Chief Superintendent." She went to her desk, lifted the flap and handed him the envelope. "Will you have coffee?"

"No, thanks. I had lunch before I came." He slid the drawing from the envelope and studied it. It was what Borden had asked for, but . . . He felt let down. The reason he'd come to Plummergen himself was because he'd more than half expected something different, something more—well, more revealing. He eyed her levelly. "This was the only one you did?"

A telltale flush betrayed her. "Oh, no. I tried several times, but that was the best."

He held out his hand. "The others?"

"I—I tore them up. You see, they weren't as good."

"All of them?" The flush deepened, Delphick's smile broadened. "Come along."

Unwillingly Miss Seeton went to the drawer, took out the

portfolio, extracted the cartoon and gave it to him. Delphick was exultant. He'd been right—and right to come himself. Otherwise she'd never have admitted to this sketch—certainly wouldn't have produced it. He examined the drawing carefully. Granted background knowledge, it told a tale and—he flicked a glance at Deirdre Kenharding—the girl's face . . . It wasn't exactly a portrait, but there was a likeness. Two men, two women in the group; he must check on the Kenharding family. Looked as if the odd mixture of intuition and observation which sprang unconsciously from her pencil when Miss Seeton's hand overruled her head had been at work again. The burning building and falling people must be some of those who had tried to stand up to the syndicate. The nest with eggs, one hatching, would be the extending of the operation. All this they knew, though Miss Seeton didn't. What interested him were the four beneath the eagle's—hawk's? ornithology was not his strong point—claws. Here, he felt a clue if he could interpret it. No use asking Miss Seeton. He doubted she had any idea what it meant herself; she'd only say it just came out like that or that she'd felt it that way but didn't know why. Borden could use the other sketch for identification—or rather, if he'd any sense, the bird's face from this one—but for himself he guessed it was the cartoon that might help. The girl—the only one of the group whose face was shown—appeared to be trying to escape. He looked speculatively at Deirdre Kenharding, who avoided meeting his eye. Kenharding . . . He'd pass it on to Borden.

He was brought back to immediate issues by Mel Forby.

"Well, Oracle, anything in all this brown study for us poor writing hacks?"

Delphick pushed the cartoon into the envelope with the other sketch. " 'Fraid not, Mel. I imagine you know about as much as we do. There was an attack on a police officer outside The Gold Fish last night and Miss Seeton went to his assistance, thereby becoming incidentally involved, so we thought it best to bring her home, as she would have had difficulty in catching the last train. The two men concerned are in custody and we hope that's the end of it."

"You hope?" challenged Thrudd. "Well, as an old comrade in arms of MissEss' who fought side by side with her in Geneva Old Town, I'd say where she is the action's likely to be. I'll stick around." In his experience chief superintendents from the Yard didn't go chasing around the countryside without good reason. Some story was in the pot and coming to the boil.

Even Mel, who had the advantage of knowing Delphick's responsible affection for the little ex-art teacher, found it extreme that he should be running errands. Then there was the Honorable Deirdre. . . . Beyond murmured "How do'you dos," she hadn't said a word, but she seemed determined to sit the party out. She wasn't local and, as a social columnist, Mel knew that old man Kenharding was on the board of directors of The Gold Fish, added to which baby brother Derrick was busy earning himself a bad reputation, had kicked over every trace and was obviously hell-bent on derailing himself. Yes, it was the Kenharding angle that interested her.

Delphick broke up the party by thanking Miss Seeton, saying that he must be getting back, that they'd let her know later whether she would be needed as a witness should the two men decide to plead not guilty and that Inspector Borden would ring her or send Haley down if anything cropped up about last night or if he had any query over the drawings.

"You wouldn't like me to cast a semiprofessional eye over those sketches?" asked Mel.

Delphick laughed. "I would not. They're strictly professional and no half measures about it. I suggest"—a slight movement of the eyes indicated Deirdre—"that if you two, with your expense accounts, really want to help, you might come back this evening and take Miss Seeton out to dinner and save her having to cook."

There was nothing, he reflected, that Miss Seeton could tell the press which they didn't already know or couldn't deduce, except the name Herrington-Casey, and since she was aware it was a confidential police matter she was unlikely to be tricked into spilling it. At that, a clever interviewer might winkle it out of one of the casino employees or The Gold Fish might deliberately leak it themselves. Leak . . . ? Could that be where the leak of Miss Seeton's name had originated? That would mean that they'd been on to her earlier in the evening, which jibed with his certainty that the attack outside had been organized from within. Would they go for her again? If Thatcher had guessed the portrait slant, he must know he'd failed and was too late. He remembered an earlier occasion when Miss Seeton's cottage had been ransacked after the police had decided all danger was over. And there was still this Kenharding angle. . . .

"You've no security here, have you?" Miss Seeton looked blank. "Burglar alarm system," he explained.

"Good gracious, no. There's nothing here for anyone to steal."

"Very wrong of you," he reproved her. "You ought to know the chief constable of Kent's been having a drive to get householders to install them and save us poor police a lot of work. I'll arrange it."

"But wouldn't it be very expensive?"

"Not to worry; we'll give it you as a present—for our own sakes." With all she'd won last night, even if they halved it with her, which was what he hoped, that was one expense there should be no difficulty over. Mel and Thrudd exchanged glances. So . . . the Oracle was expecting more trouble. Delphick nodded to Deirdre, waved to the others and took himself off, feeling pleased. The long drive and the better part of a day had not been wasted.

After Mel and Thrudd had departed, overriding Miss Seeton's protests that she would not hear of them taking her out to dinner, she turned to her remaining visitor. In spite of clothes and manner, Deirdre was, Miss Seeton realized, little more than a child. She became brisk.

"Now, you had better tell me what it is you feel you must talk to me about."

Deirdre spread her hands and her fingers writhed toward

speech. "I . . . You could help. But," she added quickly, "you must promise not to tell anybody."

"My dear, I can't possibly promise that without knowing what it is. If it's anything to do with last night that the police ought to know, naturally I should. Tell them, I mean. It would be very wrong as well as very silly not to. You'd find Chief Superintendent Delphick most kind and understanding. And discreet."

The fingers were still for a moment, then plunged. "I don't know if you know about my family?"

Miss Seeton was surprised. "No, I'm afraid I don't." Mel had called her the Honorable Deirdre Kenharding, so her father must be a lord. Weren't dukes' daughters ladies? And earls' and viscounts' honorables? Or was it the other way about? It was not, she feared, the sort of thing that she understood. In any case, she didn't. Know about the Kenhardings, that was to say.

"Father had an accident last week. . . ." Once started, Deirdre began to gain confidence, finding relief in speech. "His brakes failed going downhill near home. Luckily, except for a broken arm and bruises, Father wasn't badly hurt. And"—she looked directly at Miss Seeton—"it wasn't an accident either."

Not an . . . "How do you know?"

"The brake hose had been cut underneath. The garage told me."

"Why?" demanded Miss Seeton unexpectedly.

"Why? Because I asked them."

"Why?"

"I—" Deirdre was thrown off balance. She had only seen Miss Seeton out of her element and was unprepared to be catechized by an experienced schoolmistress. "Well, I—I knew there was something spoof about it."

"I realize that, my dear. But why?"

Deirdre laughed shortly. "If you'd been up at home last weekend, you'd know. Father was like a bear with a sore head, and when I asked about the car and what'd happened and said I thought I'd go down to the local garage and have a look at it, he blew up and told me to mind my own business and keep out of his."

"But," Miss Seeton pointed out, "you went just the same."

The girl gave a half smile. "Well, of course—wouldn't you? I'd tried talking to Mummy, but she was hopeless—just dithered and said Father knew best." She leaned forward. "They're—they're frightened. Somebody's got to do something."

How like the young, thought Miss Seeton. This sense of responsibility—ready to take on their elders' problems without even knowing how serious these problems might be. Not, she allowed, that anything, however serious, deterred them. "You don't think," she suggested, "that your father's attitude might have been only his reaction to an implied criticism of his driving ability? Gentlemen are, I believe, very touchy on the subject. I'm not implying," she added hastily on seeing the girl's expression, "that it was. Was to do with his driving, I mean. If the garage says the whatever-it-was was cut, obviously it must have been, but does your father know that?"

"Yes, they'd told him and said it ought to be reported, but Father apparently went up in the air and said nonsense, if the hose had really been cut he must've done it himself when tinkering with the car." Deirdre was scornful. "But he doesn't tinker with cars; he's got more sense. He knows nothing about them, except how to drive, and it goes straight to the garage when anything's wrong with it."

What, Miss Seeton wondered, had all this to do with last night? One hardly liked to ask outright for fear of sounding, perhaps, a little unsympathetic. "What," she asked, "has all this to do with last night?"

The girl was taken aback. "Oh, I thought you knew. Father's one of the original directors of The Gold Fish."

So that explained . . . "I do remember that Mr. Thatcher asked after your father and sent messages."

"Sent threats, you mean," retorted Deirdre.

No, really. That was too melodramatic. She had not, it

was true, cared for Mr. Thatcher's manner. But threats? A vision of her own cartoon rose to contradict her. But that, argued Miss Seeton, was pure fancy and had no relation to fact. Although one was bound to admit that it did show . . . Oh, dear. It was all very muddling. If only Deirdre had gone to the police. But there again, one could see the difficulty. If her father insisted that he was responsible, then, whatever the garage—or Deirdre—might say, one failed to see what the police could do. Nor could one very well advise the girl to go against her parents' wishes. Or certainly not without knowing a great deal more of the circumstances than one did. It was quite impossible to believe that Mr. Thatcher, someone whom one had actually met, could . . . But then it was equally apparent that the police could. Believe it, she meant. Whatever "it" was. Once more out of her element and with her thoughts squirreling in concentric circles, Miss Seeton sighed. She did so wish the chief superintendent were here. It was all so—so very muddling.

"It's all so very muddling." Miss Seeton echoed her own conclusions.

Deirdre suppressed a smile. She had watched Miss Seeton the night before, disguised in that awful war paint, gambling large sums with complete indifference and not batting an eyelash when Thatcher, as the girl now realized, had pretty well told her he knew that she was spoof. She didn't even seem a bit worried that she and Tom Haley had been attacked just after and she hadn't meant to give that chief superintendent the extra drawing either till he'd guessed and insisted; probably it had had some notes for her own use. She must be a pretty good detective, from what the papers said, and those two who were coming back to take her out to dinner obviously thought so and were hoping to get something out of her—some hope. And now to cap it all she was pretending to be muddled.

"No one would ever think you were a detective," observed Deirdre.

"No one," said Miss Seeton sharply, "would be right. Beyond doing sort of Identi-Kit drawings, when photographs are not possible for some reason, I know nothing of police work. It would be most unsuitable."

Deirdre Kenharding could hardly be blamed for her mistake. Even some members of the police force, Haley among them, insist upon regarding Miss Seeton as a subtle investigator, possibly because it fills a romantic gap in their lives. Members of the press, whatever their private views, can be excused their panegyrics since the filling of romantic gaps in the lives of others is their stock in trade.

The girl fumbled the clasp of her bag. "I don't know what the rates are for an investigation, but I won enough last night . . ." She held out a bundle of notes.

Instead of the money, her hostess took offense. "That was quite unwarranted. If I could help in any way, naturally I would." Miss Seeton relented. "But I do understand your difficulty over going to the police. They work mostly, I believe, on what people tell them and, of course, if they don't, they don't. Can't, I mean. But that you should think that I . . ." She frowned in perplexity. "I cannot imagine . . ."

It may be that herein lies the answer to the anomalies in Miss Seeton's life: that she is literal-minded is undisputed and the points at which her imagination begins or ends have always been moot. Opinions differ: the headmistress at the little school in Hampstead where Miss Seeton had worked for many years averred that Seeton caused more chaos with one good intention than the children could invent mischiefs in a year; while Sir Hubert Everleigh, on the other hand, views Miss Seeton as a victim of trouble rather than the cause, and it is for this reason, realizing that in any particular case for which she is asked to make a drawing she is likely to be at risk, that he has tried to regularize the position by paying a yearly retainer for an option upon her services. Miss Seeton has no need of specious arguments. In relation to herself she has over the years perfected the faculty, despite all evidence to the contrary, of seeing her life as she would prefer it, placid and uneventful.

This chimerical placidity Deirdre was resolved to interrupt. Intuition sent her on another tack, her hands instinctively outthrust, fingers spread and palms upturned in appeal.

"I don't know what to do."

"Couldn't you. . . . ?" But couldn't she what? Miss Seeton, too, was at a loss.

Deirdre pressed her advantage. "You see, I need advice from someone independent. I could be imagining things—I know I'm not, but I could be. Father's been edgy ever since Thatcher took over The Gold Fish. Except"—she jumped to her feet impatiently and put her coffee cup back on the tray—"of course it wasn't called a takeover: they called it 'putting in new money and ideas,' but I know there was something fishy about it. Thatcher came up to see Father and they had a row in the study after dinner—I couldn't hear what about. Mummy said I shouldn't be listening at the door, but"—she gave a slight chuckle—"what was she doing in the hall herself? Anyway, everything settled down till the Derrick business later."

"Derrick?" Faint, but pursuing, Miss Seeton was valiantly trying to follow the thread.

"Sorry. I keep forgetting you don't know about the family. Everybody's been so frightfully kind"—her tone was biting—"ringing up to say how sorry they were, just to make sure we knew they knew and had read all about it in the papers; you end by getting the feeling the whole world knows. Derrick—he's my brother—was at a party that was raided and was up at Bow Street on a drug charge. I think he was lucky to get off with only a fine." She moved back to perch on the arm of her chair. "I knew he'd gone down to London a few weeks before to see Thatcher about getting a job in one of the clubs, because he couldn't resist boasting about it. Anyway, Father exploded and made Derrick hand over his key and said if he wanted to live at home he'd have to be in before eleven, when we lock up, and that he wasn't going to have the house used as a convenience by a degenerate little—well, anyway, he called him a lot of names."

"And your brother still lives at home?" Miss Seeton asked.

"More or less, I suppose, when he's not staying with his so-called friends in London." She shrugged. "But he still sneaks into the house as late as he likes and turns up at breakfast swearing he'd come in early last night and gone straight to his room so's not to disturb anyone. I told him once he was a liar and he said that he climbs up and slips in through a window."

It all sounded most unfortunate, but not, surely, so very unusual. "After all," ventured Miss Seeton "young men . . ."

Deirdre laughed. "Now, don't you start. Mummy tried sticking up for him, saying young men always sow wild oats, but Father said boys of seventeen aren't men—and it isn't oats, it's weeds. Oh, I admit it all could be like that— just nasty and silly—if it wasn't for Thatcher." She grimaced. "I wouldn't trust him as far as I could shoot him. He came up on the Sunday after the drug affair and then Father and he had a real set-to. That time," Deirdre admitted, "I did manage to hear some of it because Father was shouting—that Thatcher was responsible for Derrick's drugging, and that he was turning The Gold Fish into a cross between a brothel and an opium den. I couldn't hear what Thatcher said, but"—she frowned, remembering— "Father didn't say anything about it afterwards—then last week there was the accident and now, as I told you, I'm pretty sure he's scared. I went to The Gold Fish to see if I could find out anything, but the barman was no help and— well, that's it," she concluded. "Except," she added with satisfaction, "that Thatcher didn't like my being there."

One thing was not clear to Miss Seeton. "Is Mr. Thatcher a family friend?"

"Good Lord, no. We'd never heard of him before The Gold Fish business."

"You don't think, perhaps," suggested Miss Seeton, "that now your brother's had a lesson, he might settle down? So many young people do silly things by way of experiment and then get over it."

"What a hope. But then you don't know Derrick." Deirdre saw her opening. "That's the whole point. If you could come up and stay next weekend—Derrick'll be there then for certain—you could have a look at all the family and see what you think. If you decide everything's all right, and I'm wrong, then all right''—She collected her handbag and stood up—"I'll see a psychiatrist."

Spend a weekend in a strange house with complete strangers? It was, of course, quite out of the question. But how to put it tactfully. "I'm afraid," said Miss Seeton, "that is quite out of the question."

"Why?" It was Deirdre's turn for an inquisition.

Why? Because . . . Well, one would have thought it was self-evident. Because . . . She found the perfect excuse. "Because it would be quite impossible to foist me on your family like that. And equally impossible to explain." She was depressed to note that the excuse sounded less than perfect—in fact, rather lame—when spoken.

"Easy." Deirdre dismissed the objection. "You taught me drawing at school."

"But I didn't."

"Of course you did." Deirdre waxed enthusiastic. "Don't you remember? You came as a temp when old Rattles was away sick; fancy your forgetting that." Her eyes danced and her brilliant smile shone out like sun on a happy landscape. "That's settled, then."

"No . . ."

"Yes. I'll call for you Saturday afternoon. Oh, by the way," She became elaborately casual. "If you see Tom Haley, you might apologize for me. Afraid I was pretty rude last night, because I didn't realize then that he was putting on an act too."

Tom Haley was summoned when Delphick, back at Scotland Yard, showed Borden Miss Seeton's sketches.

"That's the one, sir." Haley pointed to the cartoon. "That's him to the life."

Inspector Borden was dubious. "Don't see how we can run copies of a damn bird and ask for an ident. If we ever get it to court we'll be laughed out of it. How about this other?"

"Ye-es, sir." Haley was unenthusiastic. "It's like him, all right—I mean it's a jolly good likeness, but"—he shook his head—"it's not like the first. That one is—it actually is him somehow."

"Why not," suggested Delphick, "block off the rest and just reproduce the head?"

"Could do, Oracle—in fact, will do." Borden replaced the second drawing in the envelope. "And we'll try it for size on the staff at Kenharding Abbey and round the village as well. See if they know Thatcher." Haley leaned forward eagerly. The inspector noted the movement. "Right," he told the detective constable. "That can be your pigeon—better than one of the local force, who may not've seen him. But don't," he warned, "start getting pie-eyed about the place up there. None of your gin and bubbly racket and then trying to sell it to me that it was all in aid of getting the housemaids warmed up or the locals to talk. Take this." He handed Haley the cartoon. "Get it blocked off and photostated, take a couple o' copies with you and get off tomorrow."

"Can't tomorrow, sir. I'm in court in the morning and the next day."

"Damn." The inspector checked the desk calendar. "Then make it Friday—no, better still, Saturday. More natural. Young man on his tod spending a weekend in the country. And," he warned as Haley reached the door, "mind that's all you do spend."

"Yes, sir."

"And"—as a parting shot—"you stick to beer."

Altogether, Delphick congratulated himself, a most satisfactory day. He'd wormed the cartoon out of Miss Seeton, Borden had seen the light as to which sketch to use, had already known that Lord Kenharding was on the board of The Gold Fish and was pursuing that angle. Also, the A.C., whom Delphick had rung before he left Kent, had authorized the burglar alarm and had agreed to recommend

some reasonable arrangement or division of Miss Seeton's
winnings, less expenses and the installation of the alarm.
Accordingly, on his way back to town, Delphick had visited
Divisional Headquarters at Ashford, where his old friend
Superintendent Brinton, after remarking sourly that if Miss
Seeton was going to be wired for sound, at the rate of
trouble she produced they might as well rebuild her cottage
as a police HQ, had introduced himself to the sergeant in
charge of security and Delphick, having described Sweetbriars and its amenities, had extracted a promise that one of
the firms they recommended would be contacted and a rush
job put through for a burglar alarm system. A most
satisfactory day.

chapter
~4~

MISS SEETON TURNED a key with a series of dents down each side. Now, had she got it right? She read the instructions again. *Lock the main box on the stairs, after making sure that everything is in place by pressing "Tet" when the green light should show.* Well, it had. So that part was all right and it meant that the rooms upstairs and downstairs were too. Then, standing on the mat by the front door, one had to turn this peculiar dented key in the keyhole set in the doorjamb. She'd done that, so now she must close the front door, locking it behind her. She proceeded to do so.

Deirdre smiled at her. "All set? I'll take your case."

"I think so." She looked at the paper again. At the bottom it said that the kitchen was free for use at all times, but not to enter the house beyond the inside kitchen door until the alarm system had been switched off in the doorjamb, whick worked in dual control with the one at the front door. That had been arranged so that, should she be in the garden, the alarm could be on and she would still be free to use the kitchen should she want to, or take shelter if it

rained, without having to switch it off. The alarm, that was.
She sighed. She knew that it was all very well intentioned,
but it had been so much simpler when one had only to bolt
the kitchen door and then lock the front.

The kitchen door . . . Now, had she bolted it? Yes, of
course she had. Hadn't she? She'd better make sure—
Martha would be so cross. . . . She unlocked the front
door and hurried down the passage. A cacophony of bells
and a siren burst upon the village. Oh, drat the thing.
Quickly she thrust in the key and turned it in the jamb. The
bells still rang; the siren howled. But she'd . . . Why
should it . . . ? Of course—only the main switch on the
stairs would stop it. She ran up the stairs. The indoor bell
was placed above the box and clamored in her ear. Bemused
by sound, she could not fit the key. No, no, that was the
other one—this one, the flat one with ribs. That was right.
She pushed it in, gave it the half turn to "Off" and a blessed
silence descended.

Shaken and out of breath, Miss Seeton leaned against the
wall. How stupid—oh, how silly to have forgotten to
remember the one at the front door first. Now she'd start
again. To begin with, bolt the back door. She went
downstairs and along the passage to the kitchen. The back
door was already bolted. Bother. She needn't have, after
all . . . And in any case, now she came to think of it, she
could perfectly well have gone round outside the house to
see to it. She read again, turned keys again and once more
closed and locked the front door behind her. She found P.C.
Potter, who happened to be patrolling through the village in
the car which had replaced his motor scooter, backed by
Mrs. Wyght from the bakery and three of her customers, the
vicar's sister, Miss Treeves, the blacksmith and one or two
other interested spectators, clustered round the gate, while
beyond them, helpless with laughter, Deirdre leaned against
her car.

"It's certainly very effective," said Miss Treeves.

"Gave me quite a turn," declared Mrs. Wyght.

"At least you can't complain it doesn't work," gasped
Deirdre. "What a row."

The policeman came up the path. "Been having a practice, miss?"

"Oh, no, Mr. Potter," apologized Miss Seeton. "It's just that I'm not very mechanically minded and I'm afraid I got in a muddle which was first, and then which was which. Which key, I mean. I am so sorry."

"Always happens, miss, at first—it's the only way you learn it," he consoled her. "Going away?"

"Yes, just for the weekend. But Martha's got the spare keys, so if anything happens she will see to it."

"And she'll have your address, then, miss?"

"Why, no. It's only till Monday, so it wouldn't be any good sending things on."

Knowing Miss Seeton, Potter felt it might be wise for the police to have a record of her whereabouts. "Perhaps you'd better give it to me, then, miss, just in case."

Miss Seeton looked at Deirdre, who stopped laughing and straightened. "Kenharding Abbey, Little Sweepings, Suffolk," she disclosed unwillingly. She stowed Miss Seeton's case in the boot and its owner in the passenger seat, ran round the car, gave Potter and the others a vague smile, thrust the gears into first and sent the car flying down the Street.

The villagers watched it with interest; the constable thoughtfully. That weren't like Miss Seeton, to go traipsing off for the weekend. Quiet enough as a rule, unless she were on a job, and then like enough there were hell to pay. Were she on a job now? Like enough she were, after what he'd read of her doings last night. Still an' all, he'd put in a report that her alarm had kicked up and that it'd been a mistake like, and that she were off to this abbey place in Suffolk. Then 'twere up to them.

Above the village of Little Sweepings, trim, freshly painted, neatly gardened, Kenharding Abbey squatted like a disapproving dowager gone to seed; an imposing impoverishment with neither the historical association nor the capital to foist it upon the public as a Stately Home. The elderly manservant who took Miss Seeton's fiber

suitcase appeared too frail to carry it and after he had
ascended the wide sweep of the staircase in slow motion she
was relieved when they turned to the right on the gallery
that ran around three sides of the hall below, and entered a
vast dark-paneled bedroom, where he was able to lay his
burden reverently on a stool at the foot of a fourposter bed.

"Dinner is served at eight. At what time will madam take
her bath?"

"Make it seven," advised Deirdre, "before everybody's
pinched all the hot water, and it'll give you time to meet the
parents before we eat."

"Very good, Miss Deirdre. I will send Helen to assist
madam." He bowed and trembled away.

"I hope," said Deirdre, "you don't mind the odd ghost.
There's one who comes out of the paneling by the fireplace
when it's got nothing better to do. Never seen it myself, but
lots of people swear they have. Anyway, it doesn't do any
harm—doesn't throw things, doesn't say boo or clank
chains."

Miss Seeton had no bias upon the subject of ghosts and
indeed a wandering wraith fitted the somewhat discouraging
aspect of the room, where leaded windows dulled the light
but failed to hide the lack of polish and the cracks in the
heavy oaken furniture, the threadbare condition of the bed
hangings and the neat darns in the embroidered silk
coverlet.

Deirdre Kenharding read her guest's thoughts. "I warned
you on the way the place was a bit tatty." Impulsively she
caught Miss Seeton's hands and squeezed them. "I'm
awfully grateful to you for coming. And don't forget you
are a temp at Highfold School in Merriden, Sussex."

Miss Seeton did so wish that this visit need not have
involved deceiving Lord and Lady Kenharding; did so wish,
for that matter, that she herself was not involved in this
visit. But the girl had been so persuasive. And then again, if
the family had some serious trouble in which the police
could be of help, if only they could be brought to talk to
them, they could. Be of help.

A tap upon the door and, in answer to Deirdre's call,

there entered a small rotund woman with white hair drawn back into a tight bun, sharp black eyes and cheeks like withered pippins. The girl left to dress and Helen—or Hélène, as she proved to be—insisted, to Miss Seeton's embarrassment, on unpacking the suitcase and rhapsodized over Miss Seeton's best dress, which had been included "just in case." It was a semi-evening or cocktail confection and as Hélène smoothed the gray folds and examined the purple, pearl and black embroidery, she exclaimed with yearning that without doubt, without any doubt, it spoke to one of Paris. It had in fact been bought there as a parting present from someone who had reason to be grateful to the artist.

The maid led Miss Seeton to the end of the corridor, turned to the right and a few doors farther on ushered her into a conversion which must have been a source of pride in the late 1870s or '80s. She rattled the sun-faded velvet drapes across the wooden pole over the French windows while Miss Seeton gazed in awe at the biggest bath that she had ever seen. From the dais on which it stood, its eight-foot length encased in an overall ten-foot span of mahogany dominated the room and any puny human being who had the temerity to enter. Hélène advanced up the steps that led to the platform and turned a tap: it hiccuped, remained quiescent for a space, belched a cloud of steam, hiccuped again and, having cleared its system, suddenly cascaded a torrent of scalding water; the heavy metal waste cylinder, which served late Victorian England in lieu of a plug and chain, dropped into position with a clang and the other tap, on being turned, groaned, dribbled a brackish stream, then spewed forth a cold river in competition with its fellow. Descending, Hélène spread a bath sheet over the room's only chair, placed a hand towel on the seat, went back to test the water, turned off the taps, sprinkled bath salts from a cut-glass jar, returned, patted the towels and fiddled with the curtains. Miss Seeton waited patiently, recognizing from the symptoms that the Frenchwoman, like the taps, was clearing her system, in her case preparatory to speech. She trusted that neither the preliminaries nor the discourse would take long and allow the water to become cold since, true to the traditions of English comfort, the bathroom was unheated. True to human tradition, Hélène reached the door before she made up her mind, turned and crumpled her apron as an aid to confidence.

"Will madame forgive if one says to her one's thoughts?"

Miss Seeton indicated that madame would.

"Then madame must understand," she began apologetically, "that one reads the journals; and that one has known mamselle Deirdre since she was a little girl—that one has become, in effect—*comment dit?*—nurse and confidante, and by consequence one knows that there was no person with the name of Mamselle Seeton who has taught at the school Highfold. So"—she was tentative, not wishing to cause offense—"it is evident that the visit of madame here at present is—you forgive?—a little deception. Naturally," she added hurriedly, "one will say nothing—nor my husband neither—and we can only wish madame success and," she urged, "should madame have need of assistance madame has only to say and one will do one's possible—and, it goes without saying, my husband will too. Even if it must mean"—her mouth drooped and the apron suffered—"that Monsieur Derrick . . ." Relinquishing the tortured apron, she threw up her hands. "Oh, là là, there is a problem—a bad subject always, even when a little boy. Oh, là là, là là, the histories that one could tell—oh, là là, là là, là là." Unhappily she là là'd her way out and closed the door.

On her way downstairs Miss Seeton derived comfort from the knowledge that someone else in the household, apart from Deirdre, knew of the school imposture. Two people, in fact, since, presumably, the husband was included. Not only knew, but clearly approved; though the grounds for their approval were rather less clear. She was aware that her name had unfortunately been mentioned in a report of the disturbance outside that casino last week, but that, surely, could hardly be looked on as a recommendation. Then again, quite what assistance that dear old couple could give, or what circumstances could conceivably arise to render it necessary, she failed to see. But it was warming to know that if they did, they would.

The Earl of Kenharding proved to be somewhat older than Miss Seeton had expected. He came forward to greet her, hoped that she had had a good journey and that Deirdre had not driven too fast; he trusted that her room was comfortable and that she had everything she wanted. If not, she had only to say. His manner was reserved, his face tired and drawn, though the reason, Miss Seeton accepted, as she made suitable rejoinders, might well be due to pain, since his left arm was in a plaster cast and carried in a sling. His daughter regarded Miss Seeton's dress with appreciation, collected a tomato juice upon request and installed her mother and her guest together on the sofa by the fire. Lady Kenharding, a pretty woman beginning to fade but plainly a good deal younger than her husband, looked at Miss Seeton's glass.

"You're sure you wouldn't rather have something else? It seems so . . ." As with most of her remarks, the sentence petered out, giving the impression that her mind was elsewhere and that the effort involved in social conversation was too great for completion of the thought. She started on a new gambit. "Highfold—a good school, I thought, and I'm so pleased to think that Deirdre's keeping up the connection. Naturally"—the polite falsehood—"I remember meeting you there, but on those parents' days there was always such a crowd. I used to think . . ." But what her ladyship had thought was not divulged. Once more her mind had retreated into private thought and the batteries would need to be recharged before it reemerged.

At dinner the table was dominated by the empty place set next to Miss Seeton. Lord Kenharding had noted it before the meal was served and had glanced interrogatively at his wife. Receiving no better answer than a slight shake of the head, he had turned to his daughter, but Deirdre, avoiding his eye, had embarked upon a string of school reminiscences. Conversation thereafter limped and Miss Seeton's chief concern was for the aged Timson as he carried the heavy silver dishes around the table. Hélène was not in evidence—unless the excellent food was evidence in itself. Were the Timsons the only servants here? she wondered.

The atmosphere was a little easier after dinner, when they were grouped for coffee in the drawing room around a crackling log fire. The one concession to modernity, Miss Seeton marked, was an electric percolator.

Lord Kenharding, whose silence at dinner could have been attributed to the difficulty of eating with one hand, made an effort. "You're coming to the meeting, of course?"

Meeting? Some form of Sunday service, one supposed. But "meeting"? Perhaps the family were Quakers. Didn't they have "meetings"? A guest, Miss Seeton knew, should always conform. Unless, naturally, one held extreme views. And since one didn't, one should. "Well . . ." she began.

Deirdre came to her rescue. "Of course she is—that's the whole point. Besides," she added quickly to quell any attempted protest, "Miss Seeton's a great gambler. I'm relying on her for tips."

"I do wish, Deirdre"—the countess looked troubled—"that you wouldn't bet. You can't afford it and it's such a waste of money. It's bad enough with Derrick. . . ." She relapsed into thought.

"Where is Derrick?" demanded his sister. "Never known him to miss the races."

"I know, dear. That's why I imagined . . ." As usual, Lady Kenharding's imaginings were left to speculation.

"Also," continued Deirdre, "any meeting gives him splendid chances for working up a spot of trouble. Never known Derrick to miss that either."

"That's enough." Her father put a stop to the drift. "I've told you I won't have the matter discussed."

"Why not?" Deirdre was determined that family skeletons should be not only rattled but exposed for Miss Seeton's benefit. "Everybody else does, and anybody who reads the papers knows—"

"I said that's enough. Tell me," he asked Miss Seeton,

"have you found trying to teach children to draw reward-
ing? From what I remember of my daughter's efforts"—a
smile lit his face, making Deirdre's likeness to him
apparent—"if I'd been her teacher I fancy I'd have been
found hanging from the nearest picture book."

Miss Seeton laughed. "I think that learning to picture
things in the mind and to remember them is more important
than being able to put those pictures down on paper."

The reiteration of the word "picture" penetrated the
countess's absorption. "Would you like the television?" she
suggested. "We sometimes have it in the evening—and
there's always the news. Actually Timson and Hélène use it
more than we do—servants do, I think. In fact, they always
seem to know the worst before . . ." Her voice dwindled,
but Miss Seeton, pleading fatigue, made her excuses and
retired to her room, saddened to feel that this very pleasant
family should be so vexed by one renegade member, this
Derrick, who sounded no better than—her usually charit-
able mind delivered the ultimate opprobrium—no better
than a young scamp.

chapter
~5~

DERRICK KENHARDING LOLLED in an armchair. His feelings oscillated between fear and a sense of importance, and the hand in his pocket pressed a spring clip, which reassured him with a penetrating metallic click.

The noise irritated Thatcher. "Stop that. There's none of your gang here for you to call and your childish signs and passwords are hardly impressive outside your own age group." The boy reddened, to the older man's satisfaction. The young punk needed cutting down to size. Give any of these brats a job and they immediately began to see themselves sitting on thrones instead of potties. "You're quite sure you can get a man into the house without anybody knowing?"

"Told you," muttered Derrick. "Easy."

"And he can get out again without trace?"

The boy laughed shortly. "Up to him. Long as he doesn't drop his handkerchief or leave a note, it's open and shut."

Thatcher was in no mood to appreciate other people's humor. Miss Seeton had escaped from The Gold Fish without the broken hand or wrist that had been planned as an "accident" during the theft of her jewelry and winnings: a mugging that could have worn the aspect of a casual outside job and need not have involved the casino. It exacerbated his frame of mind to know that he might have been in part responsible for the debacle, having been unable to resist informing her that he had met the real Mrs. Herrington-Casey and conveying veiled threats under the guise of sociabilities. She had responded by deliberately delaying the doorman—and Haley, who could only have been feigning drunkenness, had floored both her attackers and only Morden, the driver, had got away. Added to this, the presence of the Yard's Oracle on the scene must mean that the woman's visit had been a double bluff—a trap into which he had fallen. Had Thatcher been more widely read, he might have avoided a further pitfall. Acquaintance with the works of Ouida would have warned him that "To vice innocence must always seem only a superior kind of chicanery." Without this knowledge, from what he had heard and read of Miss Seeton it was plain to him that the police used the wretched woman like a ferret, thrusting her down rabbit holes, then waiting for her to flush their quarry. She had duly put up two of his rabbits, got them caged, and there was a strong chance they'd squeal. They couldn't implicate him personally, but they would inevitably involve The Gold Fish and its personnel. He realized that it was by now probably too late to stop her making a sketch of his face, if indeed he had been right in his guess that that had been a part of the intent behind her visit to the casino, but this new move of hers . . . He scowled, reflecting on the speed at which the woman worked. No wonder her reputation stood high. This sudden intimacy with Deirdre, even to wangling an invitation to the abbey, could be dangerous. She might, where a more official approach would fail, persuade Lord Kenharding to talk, or else go to work on his wife, playing it for tea and sympathy. Also it could mean—for safety better take it that it did mean— she'd got wind of Monday's coup at Kempton and was out to drop a spanner in the works. Above all, she'd done the unforgivable—made him look a fool. He'd caught the flash of amusement on the casino proprietor's face when they'd learned the result of the attempted mugging, sensed the man's hope that the syndicate's grip had slipped. No way to keep control of an operation except by wiping out opposition. Miss Seeton's removal would keep the boys in line.

"You know which room she's likely to be in?"

"Yeah." Derrick grinned. "The haunted room. We always put guests there; it's one of the few bedrooms with central heating."

"Any difficulty about getting my man into the room?"

Derrick's grin broadened. "None." He saw no reason to tell Thatcher just how easy it would be. No reason not to let the other think he was really earning his money. "What," he asked, "do I say in the morning if she's a bit beat up?"

"Nothing. Get the man into the house, show him how to get out, show him her room, then get yourself to bed and keep out of it. She won't be there in the morning, and since you've no reason to know she was staying there, you've no reason to say a thing." He rose in dismissal from the chair at the casino proprietor's desk. "Be outside the kitchen entrance here at ten o'clock. You can lead the way on your motorbike; my man'll follow by car. But," he warned, "take it easy. I don't want either of you booked for speeding."

Fool, Thatcher apostrophized the departed Derrick. Hadn't the wit to see that when the woman turned up missing from the abbey in the morning, after a delay while the police made up their minds whether she'd left voluntarily or not, the whole Kenharding family—and Derrick in particular—would be suspect. He'd leave it to Morden to dispose of the body where it wouldn't be found easily—if at all—and the lack of it would fog the issue and delay the inquiry. Meanwhile—his mouth twisted in a smile—he wished Miss Seeton a very good night and hoped that no ghost would disturb her until her own ghost was ready to retaliate.

•   •   •

Before Miss Seeton could get into bed—in which she was comforted to see the hump of a hot-water bottle—there was a knock on the door and Deirdre arrived to apologize and explain the reason for tricking her guest into staying on for the Kempton Park races on Monday.

"But I know nothing of racing," objected Miss Seeton.

"Not to worry; I'll look after you. The point is I'm certain Derrick will be here—he never misses the races—and you must see the whole family together. I promise I'll take you home in the evening if you can't stay on till Tuesday."

Another objection occurred. "But I understand you work in London. Don't you have to be back?"

"The boutique?" Deirdre laughed. "My chief use to them is being photographed around in their outfits. When customers ask if something they've set their hearts on really suits them, I'm much too apt to tell 'em the truth, but Earl's Daughter at Local Race Meeting is a cert for most of the glossies."

"But"—Miss Seeton retreated behind a new line of defense—"I said I'd be back and Martha will be expecting me."

"You could ring up."

"She hasn't got a telephone."

"Well, surely there must be someone you could ring who could let her know."

Lady Colveden? No, Miss Seeton decided, Miss Treeves would be best. She lived so much closer and it would be no trouble for her to get in touch with Martha. And so, uncertain quite why she had, Miss Seeton eventually found herself agreeing to stay until after tea on Monday while Deirdre, having overruled objections and demolished defenses, hugged her and wished her good night.

The good-night wishes of Thatcher and Deirdre, duly noted by the powers that be, were observed to the letter if not in the spirit: nothing specific had been said with regard to the morning hours. Shortly after 1:30 A.M., Miss Seeton stirred in her sleep when a cold draft blew across the room.

To an accustomed eye objects were discernible as lighter and darker shapes, and although outlines remained indistinct, it was possible to relate position and distance.

A whitish-gray mass materialized by the fireplace, drifted forward into the room, reached the foot of the bed, floated back and vanished. The cold draft remained.

Miss Seeton opened her eyes. Goodness, it had become very chilly. Ought one, perhaps, to shut the window? She weighed the warmth of her body under the bedclothes against the cold wind on her face. Wind. Of course. A wind must have got up since she went to bed. And it was blowing in rather a nasty smell. Damp and rank. The kind of smell—well, to be quite honest, the kind of smell that one associated with graveyards. Such a pity the gardens had been allowed to run to seed so badly. The scales tipped in favor of closing the window, which inaugurated further debate. Should one turn on the bedside light? Of course, it would make it easier to see one's way. But, on the other hand, it would, inevitably, leave one very wide awake. She peered into the gloom. It wasn't really all that dark. Or rather it was, but even so, the darkness had its own relative shades. Enough, she felt, to see her way. Miss Seeton slipped out of bed, donned her woolen dressing gown and advanced cautiously toward the windows. She put her hand between the curtains, fumbled for the fastening and found—how very odd—that the windows were closed. Hélène must have shut them and then, with Deirdre coming in, one had forgotten to check and open them again. But, in that case, where was the draft coming from? And, equally, the smell? Invisible in gray wool against gray curtains, she stared about the room. A lighter shape—well, no; to be accurate it had no shape—a lighter something wavered beside the fireplace. Oh, yes; she remembered now. Deirdre had mentioned a ghost. The something glided toward the door, Miss Seeton heard the faint sound of the handle turning, there was a movement of air and the something disappeared, followed by a click as the latch reengaged. How very strange. One had always understood that ghosts could pass through doors without the trouble of opening and

shutting them. So this—how very naughty—was how
Deirdre's brother got into the house at night. Really very
thoughtless. It might easily frighten people. She was on the
point of retracing her steps when she stopped, sensing rather
than seeing another movement in the room. A thickness of a
shadow—or were there two?—crossed from the fireplace to
the bed and there was a new smell, which reminded her of
hospitals.

"What," asked Miss Seeton, "are you doing?"

A gasp of fear, the beam of a torch, pinning a man
leaning over the pillows, half turned, his mouth slack with
shock, a pad of cotton wool in one gloved hand. He jumped
toward the light. From behind it something descended with
a thwack and he fell from the beam, to disappear below the
valance. Past the torch, a hand reached out and switched on
the bedside light.

"I might've known," said Haley, "that you'd have
everything sewn up."

But at least, he reflected, this time he'd conked her
attacker, instead of her his. Bright of her to get her opponent
at a disadvantage by not being where she was expected and
then frightening the wits out of him by asking him chattily
what he was doing. How'd she intended to deal with the
type on the floor on her own? he wondered. Probably had a
pistol tucked up her sleeve or behind the curtains or what
have you. Didn't see how she could've known he was
following along behind and'd be Johnny-on-the-spot for a
bit of conking, but he'd put nothing past her—she was one
who really knew her onions, garlic and shallots.

"What d'you want done with him?" he asked.

"Done?" Miss Seeton was at a loss. So much seemed to
have happened. And so quickly. "Who is he?"

"Haven't a clue." Haley rolled the man over on his back.
"Yes, I have. Name of Morden—it was too dark to see in
the garden. Got sent up for armed robbery—that was before
the courts started to get worried—and was given a couple o'
years. Wonder," he added sourly, "they didn't give him a
pension and be done with it. We'd better—"

A light tap on the door sent Haley behind it in a bound,

his truncheon swinging loose and ready in his hand. Before he could stop her, Miss Seeton called:

"Come in."

The door opened and Haley raised the truncheon, only to let it fall, then stuff it into his pocket when a heavy iron poker faltered through the doorway, grasped in the shaking hand of a little man in striped flannel pajamas and a corded dressing gown. He was followed by a plump little woman, almost as old, with a lace-edged cap on her head, who clutched an old-fashioned flatiron. Young Haley stared at them in awe. Whose side were these supposed to be a handicap to?

"Excuse me, madam," the old man addressed Miss Seeton. "Helen and I thought we heard a bump—we sleep overhead—and voices, and wondered if you possibly required assistance."

Turning to close the door, the two old people caught sight of Haley and raised their ironmongery. The detective constable didn't know whether to laugh or cry; he longed to take their weapons away from them before they both had heart attacks.

"How very kind," replied Miss Seeton, "but Mr. Haley, who is a policeman, has been helping me."

Timson and his wife exchanged meaningful looks and nods. Hèléne noticed the unconscious Morden.

"He is dead, that one?" she asked with interest.

"No. Just sleeping off a tap on the head," Haley told her. "But if you could rustle up some cord, it'd be a good idea to tie him up before he comes round."

"If you wish, sir." Timson paused at the door. "But I venture to suggest wire would be more efficacious."

"Wire?" echoed Miss Seeton.

Timson bowed. "With respect, madam, it would seem a case where security should take precedence over comfort."

Haley laughed. One after his own heart. "Bring on your wire," he told Timson, "and we'll get him trussed and oven ready."

Timson departed. Hélène crossed to the fireplace and stood looking through the gap to one side of it left by a

sliding panel. Beyond was a small room, little more than a
cupboard, also paneled, on the farther side of which was a
hole some three feet square where the paneling was
missing. Through the opening blew a cold draft and a smell
of sour earth.

"So," she remarked. "It is by here he is come." She
turned to Miss Seeton. "And Monsieur Derrick?"

Miss Seeton nodded. "I think so. Somebody in a white
shroud opened the bedroom door and went out."

Hélène nodded in turn. "That explains itself. When I
count the linen one sheet is not there. I have told milady,
that sheet, he is disappeared. One should have known that it
was by such a trick. Monsieur Derrick has believed that if
one has seen him one will suppose that it is the ghost. But
you, you are not duped."

"Well, no," admitted Miss Seeton. "Ghosts go
through—doors, I mean—or so I've read. But this one
didn't. It turned the handle, so it wasn't. A ghost, that is."

Trust MissEss, thought Haley. If someone put him to
sleep in a haunted room and a white-shrouded shape began
flitting about, he'd have the screaming-meemies. But not
her; oh, no. If it went through the door it was a ghost, and
fair enough; if it didn't, it wasn't, and fair enough again.
Simple as that. No wonder she'd hopped out of bed and
taken up her stance behind the curtains. "Is Derrick a young
squir—a youngster with a motorbike?"

"Yes."

He spun round, to remain transfixed, staring at the vision
by the door. Deirdre, her ash-blond hair tumbling in
polished waves to her shoulders, waves which were echoed
in the flounces of her cerise and gold negligee, had the
advantage, had had time to mask astonishment at seeing
him and was able to enjoy the mental havoc that she clearly
was producing.

Juliet, he thought. Juliet. No wonder Romeo . . . Yet
when he'd had to play the part at school, a proper twit he'd
felt; killing yourself just because a girl'd died. Now
understanding dawned: ". . . For I ne'er saw true beauty
till this night" . . . "and Juliet is the sun" . . . "Then

something-devouring death do what he dare—It is enough I may but call her mine." Winged words of passion, of joy in meeting, death at parting, came crowding, clamored for expression.

Longing to tell her something of his feelings, "You wore trousers last time," Tom Haley said.

"And you were wearing shoes," observed Deirdre.

He looked down at his feet, disgraced by a pair of torn and dusty socks. He reddened. "I . . ."

"And I said that I was sorry I was rude. Did Miss Seeton tell you?"

"Miss . . . ?" Haley was jolted back to his surroundings.

Deirdre, too, came down to earth. "Hélène, what are you doing here? And what was Timson up to with a poker? I heard somebody moving about and came out thinking I might catch Derrick, but there was Timson shuffling along the landing with an enormous poker—you shouldn't've let him, Hélène, it's much too heavy—but he wouldn't stop and muttered something about wire. Then I noticed the light under this door and—" She caught her breath sharply on seeing who lay in the shadow beside the bed. "Who's that?"

"A type called Morden," Haley told her.

Before he could explain further, there was a deferential knock upon the door. Deirdre opened it and Timson entered, carrying a coil of wire and a pair of pliers. Haley moved to take them from him but the old man was unwilling to surrender them.

"If you'll excuse me, sir, I shall be able to manage quite well on my own. I am accustomed to doing odd jobs about the house."

Haley let it go. Fair enough, if that was how the old boy wanted it. But if wiring up the odd bod was just routine, just how odd did an odd job have to get about this house, before Timson found it really odd? The old man knelt, attempting to turn Morden over. He failed and Haley bent down and rolled the body onto its face. It groaned.

"Looks like he'll be back with us soon. That suit you?"

"Perfectly, thank you, sir."

"Hang on." Haley twisted the head sideways. "We don't want him to suffocate."

"No, sir?" Timson sounded dubious. He cut a length of wire, pulled the hands together behind the back and started work on the wrists.

"Well," Deirdre said, endeavoring to accept the situation with the same composure as the others, "now that you and Timson have settled Morden, whoever he is, between you, perhaps you'll explain some more."

"I—er . . ." Tricky telling her about her brother. "I don't know where to begin. It's a bit long," Haley said.

"Never mind," she told him sweetly. "We've still hours before breakfast. How you got here'll do for a start. And"—she stopped—"what's this awful smell?"

"Ether, I think. Morden had it on some cotton wool he tried to put on Miss Seeton's face. I stuffed it back in his pocket but it still pongs."

Deirdre turned to Miss Seeton in concern. "You're all right? He didn't . . . ?"

"No, my dear," Miss Seeton reassured her. "You see, I wasn't there." She had switched on a lamp and settled in an armchair by the fireplace, thankful to leave the situation to Tom Haley.

"Hélène." The girl was becoming exasperated. "For heaven's sake, put that thing down before you drop it."

"*Bien*, mamselle." The maid placed the flatiron in the hearth. "If monsieur will give me this cotton of which he speaks, I will place it beneath the coals and of a sudden we will have a fire and no smell. It will be more gay."

Without disturbing Timson, who was now securing the ankles, Haley took the pad from Morden's pocket. Was it evidence? He also found a small bottle and unstoppered it. Same smell. Fair enough; that should do. He took the cotton wool to Hélène, who pushed it into the ready-laid fire and struck a match. Flames shot up the chimney.

"*Violà*," she declared with satisfaction.

Deirdre faced Haley. "Go on," she persisted, "about how you got here."

"I followed Morden," he temporized.

"I'm getting fairly sick of Morden," she warned him. "All right, then—how did he get in here?"

"Through there." He pointed.

She went to the side of the fireplace and peered into the little room beyond. "A priest's hole—and I never even knew we'd got one. And that other opening goes down to the grounds? Brr." She shuddered. "No wonder it's cold in here."

"*Voyons* mamselle." Hélène hurried to the door. "I will make hot chocolate. It will not take long."

"Sorry about the draft," Haley apologized, "but there hasn't been time to find out how the panels work. I wanted to be able to get out again."

Deirdre fingered the edge of the opening. "And Derrick's known about this all along and never let on. The pig." Haley was relieved. So she'd realized about Derrick; at least that made things easier. "Right," Deirdre challenged him. "Why were you in the garden at all?" Though, romantically, she had an idea that she knew the answer.

The answer was prosaic. "The Yard had sent me along to make some inquiries and then they rang me they'd had a tip-off through the local man in Plummergen that Miss Seeton was staying here. I'd been asking around, but nobody down in the village seemed to know anything of Thatcher, so I decided to have a kip after tea and spend the night keeping an eye open up here."

Disappointment over her romantic notions edged the girl's voice. "We're getting somewhere at last. What did happen when you were prowling about like a guard dog?"

"Well, Derrick—your brother arrived on his bike, followed by our friend Morden in a car. They left the car down by the gates, pushed the bike up the drive and stuck it in a shed at the back of the house, then struck off to the right past a lot of bushes and lawns and whatnot. Anyway, I fell arse-over—I mean headlong—into something that scratched like a rose bed, and we ended up at some ruins which looked like a church that'd never grown up."

"The old chapel," supplied Deirdre. "It's fallen down."

"Certainly has," agreed Haley with feeling, "and not the only one. I took another purler over some odd bits of masonry. All right for the other two; they were using a torch, but I didn't dare. Anyway—" Blast this brother angle. Still no way of dodging it. Best keep it light and a bit flip and hope for the best. "Anyway, your—er—brother vanished, leaving our chum behind, and I managed to creep up close. After about five minutes—er—number one was back and told our pal everything was okay, that 'she' was there, fast asleep, to follow him, give him a minute to get clear and then carry on."

Haley cocked an eyebrow at Miss Seeton. "I didn't like that 'carry on' bit, so I thought I'd better do a bit of carrying on myself. I hared after them round a bush which nobody'd told me was a bramble, risked a quick flash with my torch and found a whacking great stone coffin with a man in armor asleep on top of it, and from the way his hands were joined, I'd say he was praying for a softer bed."

"Our great progenitor, the first earl," commented Deirdre.

"Well, under your great original's head," he explained, "the slab of the coffin was pulled back—it's on a pivot— and there were steps, so I took off my shoes, felt my way down and there we were. Derrick was on ahead with the torch, then Morden, with me padding along behind. There's just enough room to stand up if you don't mind backache."

He took a deep breath. It wasn't going to be any easier telling her the next bit. "We—er—well, we all trotted along the straight for a way and then the passage ends with steep, narrow stone steps. Up we went"—he grinned—"lucky we were all thin—and at the top the two of them had a whispered confab I couldn't hear, then Derrick disappeared through a hole at the side—that one." He indicated the little room beyond the paneling. "Morden waited a minute before going after him, me after Morden. It was black as sin in that cubbyhole, but coming through into this room you could see a bit. Morden went over to the bed, me too, then"—he chuckled suddenly, remembering—"Miss Seeton popped out from behind the curtains and said boo or words to that effect and Morden was practically knocked flat with fright, so I helped him on his way down by waving a magic wand over his head and—well,'' he finished, ''that's it.''

Deirdre regarded him in silence, thinking over the story and its implications.

The young detective was engulfed in a wave of depression. He'd done his best to play down the brother's part—no mention of ghosts and things—but no blinking it, she must know that when the police proceeded against Morden, Derrick'd be in it up to his neck. And he himself'd be chief witness. Oh, hell. And whenever he met this girl, did he have to be drunk, or in disorder? Granted he hadn't a hope, but now they were on opposite sides of the fence and . . . Hell. Finally he raised his eyes from their careful scrutiny of the carpet. Deirdre was huddled on the fender seat, smiling her warm intimate, all-embracing, dazzling smile. At him. His spirits soared. He was nine feet tall. In the seventh heaven, and still going up, he grinned fatuously back at her.

Miss Seeton watched them. So young. And so right for each other. She'd thought so at that Gold Fish place; had been sure of it later when Deirdre had asked her to apologize. And now look at them.

Hélène brought in a clinking tray and the aroma of hot chocolate filled the room. Neither sound nor smell penetrated to that Elysian meadow where Deirdre and her Tom walked hand in hand. It was left to Timson to break in upon the idyll.

''Excuse me, sir, he's done.''

Tom plummeted earthward. ''He? . . . Done?''

''The wiring. It's finished, and I trust to your satisfaction, sir. Also, the—er—man''—in Timson's world gentlemen behaved as such, while ''man'' denoted Tradesman's Entrance—''is awake.''

The detective went over to examine the old man's handiwork. ''You don't think it's perhaps a bit tight?''

''Oh, no, sir. From what I've read, and seen on the television, it is extremely simple to free yourself from bonds, with teeth or broken glass. As you see, sir, I have arranged a short length between the ankles so that he can walk. I thought it would save trouble if he could proceed under his own motivation."

"Splendid. Thank you, Timson."

Morden's one visible eye glared malevolently. "You'll hear more of this."

"Good," said Tom. "Save it till we get to HQ, where they'll want to hear more—lots more. Thank you"—to Hélène, who had handed him a cup of steaming chocolate topped with cream and a plate of cakes and biscuits.

"Where are you taking this Morden?" asked Deirdre.

"Guildford."

"How?"

"How?"

"I mean have you got a car?"

"No. I'll ring them and they'll send."

"Must you? The extension'll ping in Father's bedroom."

"Oh, I see." He did; foresaw a wealth of complications. "I suppose I could take Morden's car, though strictly I ought to leave it to be checked over where it is."

"I could run you in."

"You?"

"Why not?"

Why not? He could think of a dozen conventional reasons why not and only one personal reason why.

Watching his internal argument, Deirdre began to smile. Tom wavered and when the smile reached full force he capitulated. She drained her chocolate and stood up. "You find out how the paneling works while I put on some clothes." At the door, realization halted her. Her hands came up and the fingers began to search for words. "Derrick? Do we have to . . . ?"

From the floor Morden emitted a sound between a snarl and a laugh.

"No," said Tom quickly. "That is, not tonight. I'll have to report, of course, and then it'll be up to whoever's put in charge. They're bound to want to see him tomorrow, but"—his eyes pleaded—"it needn't affect us."

Her hands spread wide. "I hope not." She was gone.

Miss Seeton shook her head. She did hope that these two young people were not going to be foolish. It would be so easy, at a stage when they were only just becoming aware of their feelings for one another, to let this business of Derrick come between them.

The paneling mechanism proved to be simple. With Hélène and Timson each on the far side of one of the movable panels and pressing the respective knobs which released the catches, it took Tom Haley little time to find the corresponding section of the molding which worked the springs from inside. He marked both sections lightly with a pencil for future reference. In the bedroom he found Deirdre waiting for him in slacks and a sweater.

"If you'll help me push the car out of the garage we can coast down the drive and I needn't start the engine till we're clear, to save waking the parents."

"Right," he agreed, and hoisted Morden to his feet. "Can you manage?" The man refused to speak and minced across the room, hobbled by the restricting wire. Tom said good night to Miss Seeton—admitting with a rueful look at his watch that it was actually good morning and they'd likely be meeting again later in the day—thanked the Timsons and followed Morden. He shone his torch down the steps. "You keep behind," he told Deirdre, "and I'll go ahead in case he falls. But"—he stopped—"how're you going to get back in?"

"Timson can unbolt the front door and I'll use my key and creep in quietly. I'm not trying secret passages on my own."

They started down and Timson closed both panels before joining his wife to help collect the cups. He asked Miss Seeton if there was anything further they could do. Nothing, she replied, but Hélène fussed. Madame must return to bed; madame would need her sleep, and, as to that, if madame would ring the bell when she awoke, she, Hélène, would bring her breakfast to her bed. Miss Seeton, however, was firm in her refusal. These poor old dears had quite enough to do as it was and she assured Hélène that she would be down punctually for breakfast.

Back in bed, she reached to switch off the lamp. What a remarkable couple. Truly remarkable. One might well have expected the night's events to overwhelm them, at their age. But no. And they were so brave, so—so capable. She nodded a tired head. Remarkable, at their age—truly remarkable.

Timson went down to draw the bolts and Hélène set the tray on a console table near the stairs before preceding her husband up to bed. Mamselle Seeton was a woman truly remarkable. One might well have supposed that the events of the night would have overwhelmed her, at her age. But no. So brave, and capable of all. Hélène nodded her tired head. Remarkable, at her age—in truth remarkable.

chapter

~6~

DESPITE HER GOOD intentions, Miss Seeton was late for breakfast. Losing her way to the bathroom and then worrying, while dressing, over her forthcoming meeting with the boy Derrick had delayed her.

Why had he introduced that man, Morden, into the house? Apparently for an attack upon herself. But why? They surely could not be so stupid as to imagine that her very tenuous connection with the police endangered any plans that they might have. She had, of course, won a great deal of money last week, but even if they imagined she still had it, which she hadn't, they could not, reasonably, suppose that she had it with her now. Last week . . . All that hired jewelry which she had been wearing . . . That could be it. Word of that must have got about. They presumed it to be her own and imagined that, for such a visit as this, she would be sure to have it with her. Ether, after all, only rendered one unconscious for a space, and they—or rather Morden—had obviously meant to rifle her belongings. How silly of them. How very, very silly.

Silly or not, it failed to make the prospect of a confrontation with Derrick any less embarrassing. To be already in place before the other came down, to be able to nod, smile and say how do you do while engaged in eating would give the breakfaster an advantage.

As it was, Derrick had the advantage, but he lacked the knowledge to make use of his position.

With his bedroom at a distance, he could have had no apprehension of further happenstances during the night and therefore did not know that Miss Seeton was still in the house. He had been anxiously awaiting some comment upon the guest's tardiness and the subsequent discovery of her absence. Hearing the door open and taking it for granted it was Timson or Hélène, he was dumbfounded to hear his family greet Miss Seeton by name. He dropped his knife and fork and choked on a piece of bacon. His mother effected introductions and Derrick, finally red in the face and watery as to eye, mumbled an apology for having choked.

Deirdre turned from serving at the sideboard. "On a crumb of conscience?"

A warning look from her father put an end to further provocation.

The rest of the morning was one prolonged ordeal. A police car arrived at ten o'clock and a detective inspector from Guildford interviewed Miss Seeton, who, in spite of Tom Haley's efforts in dumb show to prevent her, put forward her theory that the night's alarms and excursions had been an attempt to rob her of nonexistent jewelry. The inspector then saw the Timsons and finally invited Derrick to accompany him to headquarters and make a statement.

Miss Seeton was asked if she wished to attend church and whether in that case she would prefer to walk down or to drive. Recognizing the Victorian tradition that the carriage was not used on Sundays except for the aged or the infirm, she elected to walk. Tradition also insisted, she remembered, that the stroll to church induced the proper frame of mind for the service, while the return journey was conducive to an appetite for lunch. Circumstances augured ill for both theories. Derrick's absence was not mentioned on the

way to the village, the police visit was ignored and there
was little conversation apart from remarks by Miss Seeton
on the charm of the countryside and comments, mostly
unfinished, by Lady Kenharding.

News of the police car's call at the abbey was rife and
Derrick's presence in it on its return had been observed, so
that the family's arrival at the church was greeted variously
with offensive curiosity or effusive discretion. The burning
question was: had Derrick been arrested or would he be
returning home? Granted the situation, whatever text the
vicar had selected for his sermon could probably have been
twisted to fit the occasion, but his choice from Job of "He
shall return no more to his house, neither shall his place
know him any more" was particularly unfortunate. It set
tongues wagging in whispers throughout the church and
focused the attention of the entire congregation on the
Kenharding family pew.

The family pew, below the choir, at a right angle to the
main body of the church, boasted its own private entrance
and through this the earl marshaled his party the moment the
service was over. He set a brisk pace, determined to avoid
running for a second time the gauntlet of the parish's avid
interest in the abbey's affairs. What he had gleaned of the
night's incidents, the police proceedings during the morning
and now the general knowledge of his domestic situation
brought home to him at the church, had forced his hand and
changed his mind.

The walk back was accomplished almost in silence.
Deirdre appeared to be traveling some pleasurable path of
her own. Miss Seeton could think of nothing helpful to say;
she felt that the family would be happier without a stranger
in their midst; also, she was suffering from a sense of guilt
that in some way her presence in the house had made
matters worse. The sole attempt at conversation was made
by Lady Kenharding.

"Mark, do you think perhaps . . . ?" She left it in the
air.

Her husband might not have heard, but a minute or two
later he regarded her fondly and said, "Yes, Penny, I do."

This fragment illumined for the visitor a relationship

where disparity in age was no bar to understanding, and explained the countess's superficial vagueness. Accustomed to the affinity of a mind in tune with her own, she rarely needed the full support of words to express her thoughts.

At the abbey, Deirdre, who wanted the chance of a private talk, proposed to conduct her guest round the estate, a suggestion vetoed by her father.

"As head of the house I claim the privilege of showing Miss Seeton our unrivaled collection of weeds and ruins." His daughter protested but was overruled. "You can help your mother."

"Doing what?"

"I've no idea, but failing that, you could always assist Hélène to boil the egg or whatever it is we are to have for lunch."

"I understand," said Lord Kenharding when he and Miss Seeton were out of earshot, "that you didn't sleep well."

Oh. The statement posed a problem. To admit to sleeping badly in a strange house was tantamount to criticizing the arrangements for one's comfort. On the other hand, to say that one had slept well, though perfectly true in regard to the hours when opportunity offered, would be to imply a falsehood. Perhaps if one turned the conversation, she might be able to avoid the issue.

"I assure you that the bed is most comfortable. And the hot-water bottle that Hélène had placed in it—so thoughtful—was very warming. A remarkable couple, she and her husband, so kind and—er—helpful."

"I'm glad you find them so. Hélène came originally as lady's maid to my mother and married Timson, who was then a footman. They should have retired years ago but they refuse to consider it and I'm bound to admit that what I could manage in the way of a pension would not be commensurate with their deserts. Also, we should be lost without them." Miss Seeton relaxed; the turning of the conversation had been successful. "I saw Timson last night," continued Lord Kenharding, "coming out of your room with a poker. Please," he added as Miss Seeton began to speak. "It did not for a moment cross my mind that there

was anything in the nature of an assignation. I merely
presumed that he was being—er—helpful.''

Oh. Miss Seeton realized that whatever turn she took,
Lord Kenharding would be there before her with the issue
planted firmly in her path like a gate for her to open. She
gazed for inspiration at an herbaceous border run to seed
and weed; it inspired nothing but a desire to start work upon
it with a fork. She shifted the crook of her umbrella to her
arm and pulled at the fingers of one glove; no inspiration
there. Finally she looked up at the grave face above her,
with its humorous mouth and the fine etching of laughter
round the eyes. She smiled.

"Shall we," suggested her host, "begin at the beginning?
You never taught Deirdre. Had you done so, I am convinced
she would have progressed further than the drawing of
indifferent matchstick men."

She told him of her visit to The Gold Fish and all that had
transpired since then, without interruption until she reached
the episode of the ghost's intrusion.

"Derrick?"

"Yes."

"Stupid of me. I knew of the priest's hole, naturally. We
kept it from the children while they were young—children
can be thoughtless and there would always have been the
risk of an accident or a bad fright at a party, with games
such as hide-and-seek—and to tell the truth I'd forgotten all
about it. I wonder how Derrick found out—and when." His
expression grew somber. "It explains a great deal. But I had
no idea there was another exit. They were sometimes built
that way in the older houses, like ours, where the thickness
of the walls allowed for it, but it was comparatively rare."

"You won't blame Deirdre for having spoken to me and
for telling me about the motor accident? She really was
trying to act for the best: she's very concerned about you—
and Lady Kenharding. Also, I think, though she hides it
under an offhand manner, distressed about her brother."

"No, I won't—I don't—blame her. Quite the contrary.
Youth has the impatience—you could call it courage—
which age and experience can dull. I was badly frightened

by the car business, not, I prefer to think, on my own account—in fact, I'm sure not, since my immediate reaction was anger—but out of concern for my wife and daughter." His mouth tightened. "Thatcher telephoned me with smarming sympathy on the 'accident,' congratulated me on my lucky escape, but pointed out that Penny and Deirdre were more vulnerable than I and that if I continued my opposition to his running of the casino, they might not be so fortunate. We may know, theoretically, that to yield to blackmail, whether it's against a group or an individual, is unprincipled folly, but it is difficult to apply theory when faced with fact and principles become submerged in emotion. The government which allows itself to be held to ransom for political considerations; the airline which pays up over a bomb threat; the man who pays out or keeps silent under threat—all are buying too little time at too high a price and mortgaging the safety of countless others since, once successful, such an operation will be repeated until it becomes big business." He spread his hands in a gesture reminiscent of his daughter. "I'm sorry. In excusing myself, I'm lecturing you. Unforgivable."

Poor Lord Kenharding. It was, one could see, a very awkward predicament. And of course, in theory, she was sure, he must be perfectly right. Though in practice, and if one were in the same quandary oneself . . . But here Miss Seeton's imagination failed her. Try as she might, she could not see herself as the victim of blackmail and was therefore in no position to comment. "I really do feel," she told him, "most strongly, that it would be best if you could bring yourself to talk to the police."

"I have," he replied banteringly. "And that," he pointed out, "is the object of our present exercise."

Missing his point, she continued a previous train of thought. "Also, couldn't you just avoid the casino altogether?"

"Give up my directorship, you mean?"

Well, no. Actually she hadn't meant that, since she hadn't known . . . though now she came to think of it, she remembered that Deirdre had mentioned it and she had quite forgotten—forgotten that she knew, that was to say—that he was one. Perhaps—yes, that might well be it—perhaps he needed the money.

He partially read her thoughts. "The directors' fees are purely nominal; it wasn't for that I agreed to be on the board. I hoped that if some respected names countenanced legalized gambling, we would be able to influence the way in which such establishments were run and avoid the intrusion of the racketeers." He gave a short bark of laughter. "A forlorn hope. To avoid, in fact, exactly what is happening. And as to respect for the name—they have succeeded in killing that, too, by suborning my son, introducing him to drugs and seeing that his name was blazoned in the press through a court case."

The pain in his voice drove Miss Seeton to seek for something comforting to say. "Your son is young. The young will experiment—often foolishly and thoughtlessly. And many of them are easily led. Occasionally they can become more deeply involved in wrongdoing than they intended. Don't you think that sometimes this can teach them better and make them stronger than if they hadn't? Become involved, I mean."

Lord Kenharding looked at her for several moments; then: "My dear Miss Seeton—you are an artist, and I haven't shown you the long gallery. Very remiss of me. Come along." He turned abruptly and strode toward the house, with Miss Seeton almost running to keep pace with him. He threw open a side entrance, ushered her in and up a narrow servants' staircase.

At the first flight they stopped in front of a closed door. Lord Kenharding jingled a ring on a chain from his pocket, selected a small metal tube, inserted it into a hole beside the jamb and turned it.

"Our only alarm system," he remarked. He chose another key, unlocked the door, reached in to flip a switch and stood back for Miss Seeton to enter.

The gallery, which ran nearly the full width of the abbey,

stretched before her, infinitely long, infinitely dreary, lit by
a procession of six chandeliers, in each of which glimmered
a single low-watt bulb. The sheeted shapes of chairs and
sofas, drapes drawn across the tall windows on one side and
the dark oblongs of endless pictures, with here and there a
pedestal supporting a sculptured head or bust, marching the
length of each wall, combined to produce an effect of dust
and decay. Her guide depressed another switch and, instant
magic, history sprang into glowing life. Miss Seeton gazed
in awe; moved forward in reverence.

She stopped. It couldn't be. So like, so very like, in some
respects, *The Marriage of the Arnolfinis*. Though here the
young man did not wear that unbecoming black hat, and
was turned toward the girl whose hand he held. But had Van
Eyck ever painted in England? Not that she could remember
or had ever read. Lord Kenharding resolved her doubts.

"One of my ancestors had the good sense to marry
money in the Netherlands. Painted in Bruges at the home of
the bride in 1436." So that explained how the spelling of
the name Derrick had come into the family.

Miss Seeton stared ahead down the gallery. But there
must—there must be a fortune here. "All entailed," he
divulged, "like the house and land." He shrugged. "It
would be possible to break the entail, but once you start
selling, everything goes and what have you to show for it?
My father considered it and we talked it over, but I think he
was very conscious of having succeeded as a younger son.
After all, a trust is a trust, and there is always the feeling
that the next generation may be more hard pressed than
oneself. Come on." He urged her past a painting and two
drawings by Holbein the younger. "I didn't bring you here
to browse—you can do that any time you like to your heart's
content. There." He halted in front of a large miniature.
Miss Seeton examined it. How right John Donne had been.

> . . . And, a hand, or eye
> By Hilliard drawne, is worth an history,
> By a worse painter made . . .

Then it dawned on her: this was the young man at breakfast, Derrick, in fancy dress. "Beheaded on Tower Hill for treason in 1684," said Lord Kenharding, and he moved away, followed by the reluctant Miss Seeton.

She delayed involuntarily before—yes, unmistakably—a Rubens. Next, dwarfing it in size but not overshadowing it, was a huge canvas by the same master's pupil and one-time chief assitant, Van Dyck. From the full-length portrait Deirdre's face smiled at her, framed in side ringlets, while the figure in its low-cut bodice edged with pointed lace appeared, from the swirl of the dress, only to be at pause before leaving the picture. Miss Seeton hurried to join Lord Kenharding in front of another large frame: a young man by Gainsborough, and the youth, as she had known it would be, was Derrick again; Derrick in powdered wig, lace ruffles and knee breeches, lounging in graceful artificial ease against a stone pillar improbably placed amid the roots of an overhanging tree, of which, typically, neither twig nor leaf had the temerity to throw a shadow on the face.

"Hanged for murder at Tyburn in 1782." Lord Kenharding walked on toward the end of the gallery. Disregarding the rest of the pageantry, even to ignoring the lure of Reynolds, a Cosway miniature and—no, no, she couldn't look, but yes, she was practically certain—a head by Rodin, Miss Seeton trailed in his lordship's wake.

She was confronted once more by Derrick's pretty, rather than handsome, face; the innocence of the too widely spaced eyes again belied by a sly effect in the expression; the petulant, sensual mouth; the obstinate weakness of the jaw. A Sargent, surely? And there was something in the way that the slight figure was turned back toward the artist that reminded her of . . . Of course. The Graham Robertson portrait—though this one was of a later date. So curious that while England was still indulging in the sentimental droop of Watts, Burne-Jones and Rossetti, the only portraitists of stature to emerge were both American—Whistler and Sargent. Though, admittedly, Sargent had been born in Italy of expatriate parents and had never been more than a visitor to the land of . . . Her reverie was broken by Lord Kenharding.

"Out of consideration for his younger brother, my father, who inherited, the telegram from the War Office read: 'Regret to inform you Captain Lord Kenharding killed in action the Somme September 20.' He was shot in the back by his own men while attempting to desert to the enemy." He swung to face her. "Does this answer your question in the garden about the young being taught, made stronger, through involvement?"

chapter

~7~

THE YOUNG. So many of them. Miss Seeton was surprised.
She had expected a race meeting to be attended in the main
by the middle-aged or elderly, but here the proportion of
youth seemed to be equal if not predominant. How, she
wondered, did they find the time? Or were all their
grandmothers traditionally ailing, or dead? There was bustle
and a cheerful atmosphere—so very unlike the solemnity,
the cultivated boredom, of the casino—but the sky was
overcast and there was a strong wind. She did hope it
wouldn't rain; it would be such a shame. And what
happened if it did? Did they wait for it to clear? And if it
didn't, did they put it off till another day? The riders, in
those thin blouses, were in such a very exposed position.
And then, too, the horses. If it were wet, surely they might
easily skid. Or even fall. And one could not imagine that
they would take such risks with valuable animals. She tried
to remember any paintings of race meetings, but the only
two that occurred to her were Frith's *Derby Day* and *The*

Start at Newmarket by Munnings, and in both of those the weather was fine.

"Going to bet?" asked Deirdre.

"Good gracious, no. I know nothing about it."

"Well, I'm going to back an outsider each way. The favorite'll win but it's not worth it at the odds. Won't be a minute." Deirdre, having been snapped several times by photographers, felt that she had done her duty by the shop, and putting her brother's trouble out of her mind, was determined to enjoy herself.

Miss Seeton remained by the paddock rails. She was relieved to be quit of the Abbey and had been firm in her refusal to return there for tea. Her suitcase was already in the car and Deirdre was to drive her home to Plummergen at the end of the afternoon.

Sunday had been, as she mentally termed it, an awkward day. The boy Derrick had not come home for lunch and during the afternoon Tom Haley had brought the news that Viscount Kenharding had been charged as accessory to robbery with violence, would be held overnight and was due to appear before the magistrates in the morning.

For the Guildford police, too, Sunday had proved an awkward day. The arrival in the early hours of Morden trussed with wire, although unusual, had seemed straight-forward, as had the statement made by Detective Constable Haley, supported in part by Miss Kenharding, but from there on complications had arisen, complications which the accounts given later by Miss Seeton and the two servants, although corroborating the latter part of Haley's testimony, did little to solve. What charge were they to bring against Morden? Miss Seeton's theory with regard to jewelry, which she did not in fact possess, made better sense to them than did Haley's far-fetched suggestions of abduction or murder. A holding charge of breaking and entering was impossible since Haley bore witness that Morden had broken nothing and had been introduced by the son of the house. Attempted robbery ignored the cotton wool. Attempted robbery with violence presupposed one or more of three conditions: that two or more persons were involved—but young Kenharding had left the room before the attack took place and could plead ignorance of intent; actual violence—but the only actual violence had been done by Haley to Morden; use of an offensive weapon—but was cotton wool an offensive weapon within the meaning of the act?

In any case, although it was sworn to by five people, they could not produce the cotton wool in evidence since Haley had allowed the maid to burn it. Without the cotton wool they were left with the bottle of ether, to which defense counsel would probably declare Morden was addicted, or that he used it for dandruff, or any other inanity that might plant a doubt in the minds of the jurors. Without Haley's evidence as to what had taken place in the grounds, they would have had a simple break and enter, affecting to believe, as his counsel was sure to suggest, that the youngster had been followed into the house without his knowledge. In short, they wished Haley and all his works—and his evidence—anywhere but near Guildford and took their revenge by packing him off back to the abbey to tell the family of the son and heir's arrest.

Monday morning was no less awkward for Miss Seeton. She did not, for which she thanked goodness, have to appear in court, nor did the Timsons, nor Deirdre, only Tom Haley being called to give evidence. With bail opposed by the police, Morden was remanded in custody and Viscount Kenharding was released on his father's recognizance of five hundred pounds. Despite all the Kenhardings' efforts, Miss Seeton could not shake off a feeling of guilt that she was the immediate cause of the family's present trouble.

It was no use repining. Firmly she tried to dismiss unpleasant thoughts and concentrate upon the unfamiliar scene. Horses, their initialed rugs flapping in the wind, were being led around the narrow asphalt perimeter by their "lads." Round and round and round again; surely, Miss Seeton began to fear, they would get tired. Sometimes a new one joined them, now and then one that had worn a rug retired from the procession to return later rugless and . . . Really. One knew from pictures, from the mounted police and from the horse guards, what saddles looked like. But these flat postage stamps—and not, she felt sure, even made of leather, but some synthetic product. How could anyone be expected to sit comfortably on one of those?

On the emerald oval of close-mown grass in the center, individual groups, rendered cheerful even on a gray day by the jockeys' colors, discussed their runners' chances and gave riding instructions.

That one. Miss Seeton's interest quickened. That one had quality, quite beautiful coloring and then, of course, above all, the line. Naturally, at a distance, one could not be certain of the quality, but no question, that diagonal line of silver across the little boy's chest, helping to blend the unusual combination of cerise and yellow, was most effective. Again, "boy" was really a misnomer. When one came to study them, many of the jockeys were far from being boys, it was only their size that deceived one at first glance.

"MissEss," said a voice on her left.

"Miss S.," echoed another to her right.

"Thought we'd find you here," continued Thrudd. "Martha told us where you'd gone—"

"Mrs. Bloomer to you," broke in Mel, "and Martha wouldn't've told *you* the time of day."

"All right, let's be accurate. La Bloomer gave Mel your address and knowing the poor girl couldn't manage a fashion paragraph on her own, I offered to drive her over."

"You mean you muscled in and out of the goodness of my heart I graciously allowed—"

"There's no goodness in a vacuum," retorted Thrudd. "And the day you're gracious'll be the millennium."

Who were those two? They'd hemmed MissEss in. He'd better check. Tom Haley had been combining pleasure with business, one eye on Deirdre modeling for photographs and the other on Miss Seeton. He strolled over.

"Picked your fancy, MissEss?" Miss Seeton nodded. "Right." Haley drew out his wallet, extracted five five-pound notes and handed them to her. "Here's a pony. A policeman"—his glance flicked the other two—"can't gamble on duty, so you put it on and we'll share the doings." He sauntered off, cursing himself for a fool. He'd only wanted to impress that couple and get the word "police" across. A quid'd've done it—why twenty-five, for God's sake? The neighborhood of Deirdre, he decided forlornly, was unhinging him.

"It's touching to see the faith the constabulary have in you, MissEss," observed Thrudd.

"Or lack of faith in us," suggested Mel.

"Hullo," Deirdre greeted the reporters on her return. "I think I can kiss good-bye to fifty p."

"Been plunging?" asked Thrudd.

The girl laughed. "Twenty-five pence each way on a curby-hocked nag in the hopes it'll get a place."

An idea sprang to Mel's mind. "Look, Miss Kenharding—while we're at it, what about an interview? Something on the lines of 'From Riches to Rag Trade,' and we'll get this apology for a seaside photographer"—she waved at Thrudd—"to take a picture or three. He's got to learn sometime."

"Not here, you greenhorn," Thrudd reproved her. "Can't pose for pics in the members'. Better go over to the car park."

"Right," agreed Mel. "On our way."

Deirdre looked helplessly at Miss Seeton. "D'you mind?"

"Of course not."

"Okay. You stay here till the jockeys are up, then go over to the post and I'll join you there."

"The post?"

Deirdre pointed as she moved away. "That white pole with the red circle on top. And get close up to the rails so you can see properly."

A seedy individual had pushed into the place vacated by Mel Forby. Miss Seeton edged aside to give him room. She looked behind her, searching for Tom Haley. That twenty-five pounds—a pony, he'd called it. Such a responsibility. It had been, she was convinced, no more than a gesture to

impress Mel and Mr. Banner. He could not, seriously, have
intended her to gamble with it, to—what was it?—to "put it
on." She knew no bookmakers. Nor what you did. On the
other hand, supposing that he had, and that she didn't; it
would prove so awkward if the animal won. And, in any
case, how did one? The crowd had increased, pressing
round her to discuss the horses, and she could see no one
she knew. What was she to do? A possible solution occurred
to her. It wouldn't, after all, be really dishonest and
Tom—since Saturday night she found it easier to think of
him as Tom—need never know. Twenty-five pounds was, of
course, a ridiculously large sum, but remembering the
amount that insurance company had insisted on paying her
for the recovery of those paintings in Switzerland—and,
really, quite unjustified—she could, after all, afford it. That
would make it perfectly simple. She would "put it on" and
then, supposing that the horse did win, it would be all right.
But if it didn't, she could pretend she hadn't, and then that
would be all right too. Now how . . . ? She studied the
man beside her. Not, she must admit, someone that she
would care to entrust the money to, with his checked cloth
cap and rather dirty mackintosh, but one must, in fairness,
admit that he did look knowledgeable.

"Excuse me," said Miss Seeton.

The man ignored her; intent upon his own problem, he
did not even realize that he had been addressed. He
withdrew his right hand carefully from his raincoat pocket
and let it dangle over the rail, allowing the barrel of a palm
gun to protrude fractionally between his third and fourth
fingers. In strict parlance the term "palm gun" is mislead-
ing. More in the nature of a mechanized blowpipe triggered
by a plunger which released a strong spring, it was the
inspiration of an inventor in the pay of the syndicate. With
the thumb resting upon the trigger, the gun was easy to fire
with reasonable accuracy up to a distance of six feet, its
ammunition being a single dart contained in an airtight
capsule which broke when the plunger was pressed. Two
suborned scientists spent more than a year perfecting this
cartridge, basing their experiments upon the anaesthetic

injections for cattle and the tranquilizer darts for wild
animals such as the New York police tried in an attempt to
control the packs of stray dogs that roam the slums of
Brooklyn. The two chemists finally arrived at a modified
solution of an opium derivative "frozen" into a splinter
with a needle-sharp point, which, owing to its pain-killing
propensities, was comparable to the bite of a stinging fly.
The splinter would evaporate quickly when exposed to air
so that, apart from the pinprick in the animal's leg or
hindquarters, the "wound" would be virtually undetect-
able. The result of the local anaesthetic would be equally
hard to discern: the horse might show initially a slight
excitement, but no more than many race horses do normally
when cantering down to the start. Some ten minutes after
the "injection" there would be a faint lethargy in the
affected muscles, lasting only for a few seconds, which
could be attributed to change of leg or an unevenness in the
going. These few vital seconds could lose the race and over
a period the syndicate had reaped ample dividends on the
money invested in research.

An announcement over the PA requested "*Jockeys get
mounted, please,*" and Miss Seeton saw the rider of her
choice, in his cerise and yellow with the diagonal silver
band, thrown up onto the top of the horse by the gentleman
beside him. Discussions between owners and trainers were
over, instructions had been given and the favorite, Fancy's
Folly, with the jockey up, was being led around, preparatory to leaving the paddock.

Now was the moment. The seedy individual tensed,
ready for action. He brought his hand up and, as Fancy's
Folly came abreast, aligned the palm gun with the colt's
hindquarters. His thumb stiffened on the plunger and—

Miss Seeton tapped him on the shoulder. At the all-too-
familiar touch, the man jerked his hand down, prepared to
bluff it out that he weren't doin' nothink, but he was too late
to stop the pressure of his thumb upon the trigger.

The scientists who had invented the dart had not fully
evaluated the potential of their brainchild. Its penetration of
horse's hide and its efficacy upon the animal had been nicely

calculated. Its power to puncture tanned leather and its effects upon a human being were unknown equations, equations which, thanks to Miss Seeton, were now to be resolved.

The man swore with fright, letting the gun fall, as he felt the dart pierce his shoe and become embedded in his foot. Ducking away from the hand on his shoulder, which had not been followed by its usual corollary, "I'm taking you in," he bolted.

Oh, dear. Miss Seeton felt guilty. That poor little man. She'd startled him. One forgot that many people took racing quite seriously and no doubt he'd been absorbed in studying—form, she thought it was called. And now she'd disturbed his calculations. Oh, dear. Also—she stooped and picked up the palm gun—he'd dropped his . . . Would it be some form of pocket camera? She looked about, but in the throng of raincoats she could not distinguish the rather dirty one topped by a checked cap which she sought. Never mind; there must be a lost property office somewhere. She dropped the object into her bag. Deirdre might know. Or if not, she could give it to Tom. He'd be sure to arrange things.

Tom Haley was doubtful as to his next move. Temporarily undistracted by the presence of Deirdre, he had been keeping a close if inconspicuous watch over his charge. He had seen her accost the man beside her and for one happy moment had thought that she was going to clap the bracelets on him herself, but when the little runt had scarpered it had dawned that MissEss was merely putting the finger on him, and as the grubby raincoat dived into the crowd, Tom jumped forward and fielded him.

"In a hurry, chum?"

The man tried to squirm free. "'S right. Ah'm lite fer a dite."

The pathos in the poem failed to move. Tom Haley kept his grip. "I'm sure she won't mind waiting the odd minute."

The other aimed a wicked kick; then an expression of

horror began to dawn upon his face. The backswing had
been easy, all too easy, while the forward sweep went on
and on and on, the hip disjointing painlessly, the muscles,
sinews, flesh and skin all parting without hurt; fully he
expected to see his unshackled leg go sailing past him like
the loosened wheel of a speeding car. In common with such
a car, he now collapsed upon his axle.

"Kerrist," he bleated. "Me bleedin' leg—it's gorn."

"Trouble?" inquired a uniformed member of the racecourse police.

Tom Haley showed his credentials. "This man—" he
began.

The constable looked down. "That's no man—that's
Frank the Finger. What you been up to this time, Fingers?"

"An ambilence," wailed Fingers. "Get me to orspittle
quick. Ah'm dyin'."

"It's a nice thought," commented the policeman. "What
makes you think so?"

"Ah'm pizened."

There was a slight change in the attitude of the two
officers, a stiffening of mental antennae. "Poisoned?"
queried Tom. "Who by?"

"Done it meself," mumbled the man on the ground,
"with that blarsted—" Despite his fright, belated caution
stopped him.

"I'll whistle up a wagon," muttered the uniformed man.
"He looks pecu' an' that's a fact." He took his personal
radio from his pocket, reported and asked for an ambulance
to be sent.

"So you went and poisoned yourself, did you?" asked.
Tom. "What with?" Fingers' mouth tightened mulishly.

The policeman replaced his radio. "Please yourself, but
there's not much they can do for you 'less they know what
you took."

"The orspittle'll set me to rights."

"Don't be green. How can they if they don't know what's
wrong with you? Could take 'em days to find out—like as
not till after the postmortem."

"The . . . ?" Fingers clutched the officer's trouser leg. "Look, Ah'll be orl right, won' I?"

"How'd I know?" He surveyed the sitting man dispassionately. "From the look of you, I'd as lief not be in your shoes—or out of 'em."

"Kerrist," whined Fingers. "It's gettin' me arms now— Ah carn't feel 'em." His hand lost its grasp on the trousers; he tried to raise both arms and failed. "Look, yer gotter 'elp me. Ah carn't sing; if Ah do they'll do me."

The policeman shrugged. "Up to you. Die what way you like—all one to me." He looked up on hearing the approaching wail of an ambulance.

Fingers appealed to Tom. "Look, that a fac', they carn't do nuffink at the orspittle 'less they know?"

Tom duplicated his colleague's shrug. "Can't give you an antidote till they know what the poison is."

"But Ah dunno meself," moaned Fingers. "It's fer 'osses, not 'umans. Look." The paralysis had risen and he turned his head with difficulty. "If Ah give 'em some o' what Ah got, would it 'elp?"

"Should think so," encouraged Tom. "Make it quicker anyway."

The uniformed man had cleared a way through the crowd for the ambulance and two bearers were approaching with a stretcher.

"Look," muttered the terrified Fingers. "Little box in me right pocket—couple of them darts left. Make like yer givin' 'em a 'and up wiv me and give it to one o' the blokes. But for the love o' Kerrist," he warned, "don' let nobody see yer snitch it."

Tom carried out the instructions, palmed the small case from the raincoat pocket and sauntered over to speak to the driver of the ambulance, while the bearers settled Fingers on the stretcher and laid a blanket over him. Tom had only taken a few steps when he was halted by a sound like the crack of a whip. He swung about in time to see the figure on the stretcher convulse and then collapse. He ran back, his colleague darted forward and the two ambulance attendants stood for an instant, petrified, until training told and the front bearer, seeing the hole in their patient's temple, flipped the blanket over the corpse's head and both men in a concerted surge thrust the stretcher into the ambulance, leaped in after it and slammed the doors. A moment later the engine roared as the driver accelerated away along the path left by the sympathetic crowd.

The whole incident had happened so quickly that none of the bystanders had realized its significance. The uniformed man was reporting by radio and calling for reinforcements, although there was little chance of finding the marksman in the press of people and the police had no wish to start a panic in the members' enclosure. Tom decided that for him the safety of his charge must take priority and he hurried back to the paddock rails. Miss Seeton had gone.

Perhaps up here? Miss Seeton had passed the unsaddling enclosure and was ascending the slope to the stands. In front of her across a wide lawn—how, she wondered enviously, thinking of the continual fight with plantain, buttercup and daisies at home, did they manage to keep their turf so immaculate?—and visible above the heads of the crowd was the winning post of which Deirdre had spoken, and yes, over there on the right were a lot of very busy gentlemen leaning over a board fence, who must, she felt sure, be bookmakers. Approaching Tattersall's rails, she experienced a qualm. How did one place money on a horse of which one did not know the name? It would sound, surely, so very—well—odd to say one wished to back a blouse. Most people, she noticed, carried a small paper booklet which they frequently consulted and on which they jotted down notes. Of course. Miss Seeton searched in her handbag and found the race card Deirdre had given her. She checked the time and found the page. Studying the list of runners, she discovered that the colors were mentioned at the bottom in smaller print below each horse and—how encouraging none of the others had cerise or silver—this one must be hers.

204   OOMPAHPAH. 4 7 0 (6)
   B g Trumpeter—Papa's
   Daughter
0/000-0 **Mrs. F. Santoyne (Major V.**
   Coldwort Newmarket)
   C. Bells
   CERISE and YELLOW
   halved. SILVER sash

B g? Would that be what they called a tip? The children at
school, she remembered, had often referred to things of
which they disapproved as n.b.g., so presumably this must
mean the opposite. She scanned the rest of the entry. There
was a Fancy's Folly, which was Ch c; there were B c's, a Bl
c and a B f—another term she recognized from her teaching
days—but hers was the only B g. Really, it was quite an
omen. With mounting confidence, Miss Seeton approached
a bookmaker and offered her sheaf of notes, only to be told:

"No cash here, lady—though there." He pointed.

Drops of rain began to fall, slanted by the wind. Time
and her confidence were both evaporating. Anxiously Miss
Seeton pushed her way through the opening to Tattersall's
ring. A beaming red face with a raucous voice and a bold
sign on a sort of music stand

ᵧₒᵁRELⁱ^{ñe's}ABLE
REX

caught her attention. She took her place behind two men
who handed money to a small wizened man beside the
bookmaker. On a board was chalked:

8-11	FANCY'S FOLLY
7-2	GARTER NIGHT
8-1	ARGOVIN
100-6	EMPIRE'S TALLY
20-1	BAR

Hers wasn't there. Nor—she glanced at the race card—was there a horse called Bar. Perhaps that was in another race. She nerved herself to say the word Oompahpah—really, such childish and embarrassing names they gave these unfortunate animals—but when her turn came her courage failed her and she handed over the five five-pound notes, placed her finger on the list and said simply:

"I wish to put this pony on that horse."

"Right, ma'am, you're on at twenties." The clerk scribbled in a ledger and handed her a numbered card.

The rain was becoming heavier. She did hope that it would prove to be no more than a shower. She put the card into her handbag and opened her umbrella.

"Has Deirdre deserted you?" Miss Seeton looked up to find Lord and Lady Kenharding beside her.

"We saw you go through to Tatts," explained Lady Kenharding, "and thought perhaps you were lost and so . . ."

"Instead of which," said his lordship, who had observed Miss Seeton's transaction with Reliable Rex, "we find you very much at home and in control of affairs."

"It's only a few minutes to the off—would you like to come up to the stands with us?" suggested Lady Kenharding. "You get the best view and it's more . . ."

"How very kind. I would have loved to. But I promised to meet Deirdre by the post."

"Then you'd better get along," Lord Kenharding told her, "or you won't get a place on the rails and you'll miss the race."

Gratefully Miss Seeton bade them good-bye and set off, a little pleased with herself. "Very much at home," Lord Kenharding had said, and "in control." Really, it had been foolish to allow oneself to worry so. It had all been quite easy and the vernacular of the racecourse was perfectly simple to understand if one applied one's common sense.

Lord Kenharding frowned after the retreating little figure mushroomed under its umbrella. Abruptly:

"Penny?"

"Mm?"

"How do you feel about that emerald brooch of yours?"

"With all those diamonds and the pendant? Well, it's always in the bank, so I don't actually feel . . . Why? Were you thinking of . . . ?"

"It had occurred to me. I stood surety for Derrick this morning to the tune of five hundred pounds we can't afford." He stopped, then let his breath out in a sigh. "Do you think he'll jump his bail?"

She pursed her lips. "I'm afraid he might if he can think of anywhere to hide. Or his new friends . . ."

"Quite. And as surety for ourselves that brooch is about the only thing we have left that's not in the entail."

"So you thought Fancy's Folly? she asked. "But it's odds on, and . . ."

"Er—no." He was embarrassed. "You couldn't see over her shoulder, but our schoolmarm has just sprung a pony on Oompahpah. I must admit it made me feel like springing the equivalent of the bail money and putting a monkey up behind it."

"Five hundred? On Oom . . . ?" Lady Kenharding was shocked. "But, Mark, it couldn't get a place in a two-horse match."

"I know, so why did she do it? She waits till Deirdre's out of the way, then slips in here and plunges on an outsider. Why? The Jockey Club prefer to run their own affairs, but have the police got wind the race has been rigged but can't prove it, so she thought she might as well pick up something on the side? Don't be fooled by all the innocence, Penny. That little woman knows exactly what she's doing, though she'll never admit it. 'I know nothing of police work,' " he mimicked. "Merely happens to hold a rather high position at Scotland Yard, for which innocence and idiocy are not the criteria. And 'I know nothing of racing,' but enough to call twenty-five pounds a pony and to point to the name of the horse instead of saying it, in order not to tip off anybody around." He laughed. "Forget it, Penny. She's getting me hypnotized. Come along, we must get to the stands. There isn't much time."

She caught his sleeve. "About the brooch . . . I think

I've really always looked on it as something you gave me to put by for a rainy day."

"Of course. I said forget it, Penny."

"But, Mark." Lady Kenharding was inspired to finish her second consecutive sentence while raindrops pattered on her upraised face. "This is a rainy day."

chapter

~8~

LORD KENHARDING HAD not been the only person to be
interested in Miss Seeton's wager. A man had sidled as
close as he could, but without being able to see which horse
she had indicated. Point was, had the fuzz cottoned that
Fingers had mucked the job on the favorite, or not? Was the
old bag splashing her money on Garter Night thinking the
original deal was still on, or was she buying loose cash on
Fancy's Folly, knowing it would now win? Much good it
would do her; she'd never collect. The word was out on her
and she'd had hers. But not till after the race. Enough was
enough. Bumping Fingers before he could sing was all the
market'd take for one afternoon. The man puffed his chest:
neat a bit of shooting as you could wish on short notice and
not a soul'd cottoned 'cept the stretcher men and the fuzz.
Orders were *this* one was to be an accident—one of those
things. Member of the public caught in a teen-age riot. Too
bad; nothing personal. Though from what he'd heard,
young Kenharding had his own thing to settle with her and

it'd be personal as hell. Not his show anyway. All he'd got
to do was keep alongside and mark her for the boys when
they started in. He came abreast.

"Give you the winner, ma'am?" he insinuated.

She smiled and shook her head. "No, thank you," said
Miss Seeton. "I already have it."

There. There was a little gap. The rain had eased. Miss
Seeton closed her umbrella and managed to slide into a
small space against the outside rails. It wasn't quite so close
to the post as one had hoped, but farther along there was no
room at all. Deirdre would be sure to find her here.

The man following her smiled sardonically. Mark her?
With her brolly, she'd marked herself. About the only gamp
in sight, except for the bookies'. This old trout'd wrecked
as nice a little setup as you could wish. And snaffled the
gun. Well, now she was set up herself and they'd get the
gun back when she got hers. He hoped the lads'd had time
to get the cash on Fancy's Folly, though at odds of 11–8 on
and probably worse by now it'd mean one hell of a spread to
cover what they'd staked on Garter Night. No wonder the
bosses were flippin' mad.

High up in the stands, Thatcher relaxed. It had been a
rush, but the money was on and they were covered, though
the odds had finally shortened to 6–4 on. Damn that woman
to hell. Below him he saw the Kenhardings take seats near
the front. He was surprised. You'd have thought, after the
magistrate's court this morning, they wouldn't have shown
their faces. Noblesse oblige, a stiff upper lip, he supposed.
Well, he'd soon be taking the starch out of them for
bringing the police in. Deirdre appeared, looking worried,
glanced around, then hurried to join her parents. Thatcher's
lips curled. She'd have plenty to worry her soon enough.
An idea was born. Young Kenharding would have to be
taken out of circulation after this Miss Seeton's unfortunate
demise and the boy's ducking his bail would hit his lordship
where it hurt. For the future? Probably get rid of him—

Derrick was a fool and too full of himself to learn—but keep him on ice as long as he was useful as a lever against his father. Then later, when things had died down, snatch the girl. That would teach Kenharding to toe the line and be an object lesson to others all around. With both the children under wraps, the parents would have to dance to any tune he called. The manager of The Gold Fish, too, was showing signs of getting restive; another matter that must be dealt with. And all of it stemmed from the Seeton woman. Once she was eliminated, things would settle down to normal. How the devil had she got on to Fingers in the first place? At least that had been dealt with promptly and now it was merely a question of dealing with her—and getting back the gun.

". . . *in the stalls now,*" announced the PA, "*all except Argovin . . . no, Argovin is in. They're off.*"

A bell sounded and Thatcher raised his field glasses to concentrate upon the race.

". . . *no, Argovin is in. They're off.*"

A bell rang and expectantly Miss Seeton leaned forward and looked to her left, only to find herself staring into the face of the man who had so kindly offered to give her a winner. He—in fact everybody, she now realized—was facing the other way. She looked to her right. Nothing.

". . . *early stage of the race there's Fancy's Folly showing most speed, followed by Garter Night on the stand rail, and just behind the leaders in a group I can see Ferndale, Empire's Tally and behind Empire's Tally, Argovin . . . and at the rear of the field Grass Seed and Oompahpah.*"

Now in the distance Miss Seeton could see moving specks.

". . . *Coming up now towards the five-furlong marker*"—a different but equally indifferent voice had taken up the commentary—"*it's Fancy's Folly in the lead from Garter Night, followed by Ferndale.*"

The dots increased in size, the murmur grew, swelling to a roar as the horses—yes, at last she could see them—came pounding down toward her.

Now she could appreciate the reason for those postage stamp saddles: they were merely a decoration, in deference to convention and not for use at all, since the riders stood crouched with heads down by the horses' necks and their behinds well up in the air. Several of them were quite close, just the other side of the farther rail, but hers—yellow, cerise and silver—wasn't there. Oh, yes, there it was—right on the other side and rather far behind, the silly animal. Around her everyone was shouting encouragement to their choice and, infected by the general excitement, Miss Seeton shouted too.

"You there," she piped, "come along, hurry up—oh, do be quick."

Unthinkingly she waved her umbrella to attract Oompahpah's attention. The wind caught it, turned it inside out and tore it from her grasp. It landed on the course in front of Fancy's Folly. The favorite swerved, bumped Garter Night and almost fell. Garter Night stumbled, then recovered, while behind the two leaders swearing jockeys fought to pull their own mounts clear.

The suave voice of the commentator quickened. *"Fancy's Folly's down—no, he's recovered, but Garter Night . . ."* His words speeded to a gabble that was drowned by the roar of mingled rage and excitement from the crowd.

On the far side Oompahpah pursued its lethargic way until—whether in answer to Miss Seeton's plea, spurred by the zoological specimens that she and Lord Kenharding had placed upon its back or, accustomed to trailing in the rear and, with no horse in front, deciding that it had overdone indolence and been left too far behind the field—to the astonishment of its jockey, its owner and its trainer, the bay gelding suddenly shot forward like a released arrow to win by half a length.

•   •   •

"Better get her out of this before she's lynched."

Thrudd Banner grasped one of Miss Seeton's arms, Mel Forby grabbed the other and the two reporters hustled their bewildered victim back toward the stands.

"But . . ."

"No buts. Come on."

Miss Seeton held back. "But please, Mr. Banner, don't I have to give this card"—she opened her handbag—"to Mr. Rex—he's a bookmaker in what I think is called Tatts—because . . ."

Thrudd looked down at the card she held. "No, you don't have to give that to anybody. The race went up the spout owing to a"—he grinned at her—"shall we say a contretemps, and some paralyzed donkey disguised as a horse won it. Not even its owner backed it."

"But I did. Or rather I did it for Tom—Mr. Haley, that is—because of the colors, you see," she explained.

"No, I don't, but never mind. If you really backed this Oompops or whatever because of the length of its eyelashes, we'd better go and collect quick before someone gets the idea you threw the brolly on the course to save your ten p." Thrudd veered left, guided Miss Seeton among the crowd, hustled her through the gap into Tattersall's and up to Reliable Rex.

"There you are. Collect your ill-gotten gains and then I think you're better out of this."

Miss Seeton handed over her card. Reliable Rex looked at her for a long moment, put his hand in his satchel and silently began to count notes into her hand. As the counting continued, Thrudd's eyes widened; even Mel's faith in innocence was shaken. They watched until five hundred pounds had been handed over and Miss Seeton began to expostulate. Surely, she thought, it seemed so much—too much. . . . Thrudd cut short her protest, whisked her away and headed for the car park.

"And to think," he addressed Mel over Miss Seeton's head, "that only a couple of weeks ago I did an article on lack of corruption in the police."

"Oughtn't I," ventured Miss Seeton, "to collect my umbrella?"

Mel and Thrudd had found Miss Seeton too late to see the incident which had affected the outcome of the race, but the mangled remains of metal and black nylon still lay beyond the rails and the overhead remarks from the crowd discussing the event—"A brolly" . . . "A bloody gamp," . . . "umbrella, thrown on the course deliberately"—combined with Miss Seeton's present lack of her usual armory, had given them a rough idea as to what had taken place.

Mel laughed. "Your umbrella? On the whole, no, and if anybody asks, I'd swear blind it isn't yours if I were you. Forget it, Miss S. You've got enough there to buy a few dozen more."

Tom Haley, too, hearing the repeated mention of an umbrella and drawing his own conclusions, had decided to search for his charge by the rails. Pushing his way through the throng, he saw her returning with her two escorts from her visit to the bookmaker.

"There you are," he exclaimed with relief. "I was afraid I'd lost you."

"Not lost," observed Thrudd sourly. "Just gone before— and to a very pretty tune at that."

"There's been . . ." Haley was in a quandary. He thought that Miss Seeton was unaware of Fingers' death, and that it would be healthier to get away—though it was awkward, her being there as a guest of the Kenhardings. Also, he did not wish to tip off the reporters. "There's been a bit of a development," he said lamely. "I think it's time you left."

Three hearts that beat one thought among them. "You're overruled, Miss S. We all think you ought to go."

"But," Miss Seeton pointed out, "I have to wait for Deirdre. She's driving me home."

Deirdre. Tom Haley brightened. "We'll find her and I'll follow in my car just in case."

Thrudd became alert. "In case of what?"

The announcement of the runners for the next race saved Tom the necessity of answering and their route to the car park, which crossed the main stream heading for the paddock, made conversation impossible.

The car park appeared to be deserted. As they approached the first line of cars, Tom heard a metallic click. Another. Then another. The sound teased his mind. He couldn't remember . . . but it registered a warning. Yes—*The Police News*. There'd been an advice that some of the young hoodlums used a small metal spring to signal to each other, especially when ganging up for a fight.

"Wait," he commanded. The others halted in surprise. "Back—quick." He turned, but behind them a man lounged, grinning, a pistol dangled in his hand. Miss Seeton's erstwhile tipster had played the good shepherd and now, having penned the lambs for slaughter, could relax and linger to enjoy the butchery.

The incessant menace of the metallic clicks, which by now filled the air and exacerbated the nerves, was cut by the sound of shattering glass. A score of youths sprang from behind the cars. Windows and windshields smashed under coshes; expensive coachwork dented and buckled beneath heavy boots. An attendant came running, was sapped to the ground and kicked unconscious as he huddled for protection. Farther off, other attendants, seeing the odds against them, ran for the fence, scrambling or vaulting over it according to their age and prowess, in a race to summon help.

The young men, their appetites whetted by the mutilated vehicles and the crumpled figure lying on the grass, fanned out in a semicircle to close in on their quarry.

Held inside the car park by the threat of the gun and the knowledge that any attempt to escape would accelerate attack, for the first time Tom Haley regretted being in plain clothes. No personal radio, no whistle, no truncheon— nothing. Instinctively he and Thrudd had backed the women against the fence, to stand in front of them at bay, while Mel, deciding that in the circumstances a woman's arsenal

held but one effective weapon—her throat—screamed and
screamed again. Miss Seeton was silent, shocked beyond
words that these—these ragamuffins, really little more than
children, albeit children who she perceived were quite
beyond control, should be led by the Kenharding boy,
Deirdre's brother Derrick.

Once he had seen that his victims were safely hemmed in,
Miss Seeton's tipster pocketed his pistol and decamped.
Hopped-up young fools. Couldn't resist working themselves up for the kill by smashing whatever lay in their path
and making enough row to raise the whole police force of
the county. God save him from amateurs. Maybe the bosses
were right to play it this way, but give him a quick
professional kill and a fast get-out every time.

The county police, or at all events those members of the
force on duty at the racecourse, had indeed been raised by
the noise of the damage to the cars coupled with Mel's
screams, and also by the car park attendants. They were on
their way, calling for reinforcements as they ran, but to the
beleaguered quartet the situation looked hopeless. Mel's
shrieks appeared to drive the youths into a frenzy of
expectation, encouraging them to prolong the torment.
They yodeled back in imitation. Two darted forward and
knocked Thrudd to the ground while Mel, who had removed
one shoe for armament, slammed at their faces with the
heel, giving her protector time to regain his feet, kick one of
his assailants in the groin and deliver an uppercut which
floored the other. Tom Haley, whose police training stood
him in better stead, with an armlock on one youngster,
hooked the legs from under a second, getting one foot on his
neck, and was butting a third in the face when Derrick
Kenharding came at him with a knife. Tom swerved to
avoid an upward thrust for the abdomen, the arm of the boy
he was holding snapped, to a howled accompaniment, and
the blade only pierced Tom's hip. Derrick retrieved the knife
with a grin of triumph. His adversary was off balance and
defenseless; he slashed for the throat. Behind Tom Miss
Seeton reacted in desperation and swung the only weapon
that remained to her, her handbag. The stout, old-fashioned

leather, with its sensible clasp preventing her on this occasion from showering her winnings abroad, caught Derrick full in the face, deflected his aim, and as he staggered, momentarily blinded, the knife blade buried itself in Tom's shoulder.

chapter

~9~

TOM HALEY GAZED about him. Slowly the picture of his surroundings settled into focus. Beside him, opposite him, were rows of iron bedsteads with figures lying or sitting, some with earphones on, and over all the pervasive smell of . . . What was he doing in a hospital ward, for God's sake?

Somebody'd boobed someplace. There was something important he had to . . . Tom tried to get out of bed. His right arm and leg helped to push him up in the bed, although the position was lopsided since his left limbs refused to cooperate. There was pain. It had a dulled edge but carried a warning that should he take liberties, it could sharpen and become acute. He looked down at himself. His left forearm was strapped across his chest and, raising the bedclothes, he found that his left thigh was padded and swathed in bandages. He made a determined effort. As though he had pressed a television switch while the tube was still warm, his vision of the ward tilted backward, spun and clicked into place on a different channel. Deirdre Kenharding's face in

close-up. Tom relaxed carefully, controlling his breathing,
fearful lest further movement should again change the
program. Deirdre smiled. The focus was good, the picture
steady; this program was definitely on. Well, he couldn't go
on lying there gawping at her. Say something. Some neatly
turned phrase in greeting, casual, preferably witty, just to
test if she was real.

" 'Lo," muttered Tom.

"Oh, good." Deirdre laughed in relief. "I wasn't sure if
you were really with us—you look a bit wonk-eyed. They
didn't want to let me in but I said . . ." Well, never mind
what she'd said; anyway, it had got her in. "How're you
feeling?"

"Fine," lied Tom.

"Well, you don't look it. I . . ." Her hands came into
play. How did she—how could she put it? "I'm desperately
sorry about Derrick. He must've been mad—or drugged, I
suppose. But even so"—her fingers played a tortured
accompaniment—"to try and kill you and Miss
Seeton . . . I just don't . . . I can't . . ." Both hands
and voice yielded to incredulity.

Miss Seeton? MissEss? Derrick? The events of the
afternoon swayed through his mind in an obscure panorama
of flashbacks. Tom Haley began to fret. "MissEss," he
mumbled. "Sh' all right?"

"She's fine. Those two reporters are driving her
home—"

Tom roused himself. "No," he interrupted.

"Yes. You see, I was going to take her back, but with all
that happened and coming to the hospital and having to wait
and everything, I couldn't, so they said not to worry, they'd
run her down to Plummergen and—"

"No," repeated Tom. "She's my reshponsh—" He
shook his head, winced as the pain in his shoulder flared,
made a determined effort: " 'shponshibility," he stated
firmly. He had an uncomfortable feeling of *déjà dit*, though
no one, this time, could accuse him of swilling gin and
bubbly.

Deirdre laughed. "Don't be silly. You couldn't drive

anyone anywhere at the moment. You lost an awful lot of blood and that had to be replaced and your arm and leg had to be stitched up and they shot you full of all sorts of things and you were out for the count—that's why you're still woozy."

Memory of the fight in the car park took on a keener edge and with memory came a keener edge to the pain in his thigh and shoulder. He remembered that last moment as the knife slashed for his throat; remembered knowing he'd bought it. But although his brain might be less trammeled, his mouth still retained an overplus of furred tongue. "How'd he mish me?"

"Miss Forby told me—she saw it. I thought she'd been hurt herself because she was limping, but it was only she'd lost the heel off one of her shoes. You were in front of Miss Seeton, and you'd knocked out three of them." Deirdre's eyes shone with pride. "Then when Derrick went for you with a knife, Miss Seeton slammed him in the face with her handbag."

That was the second time, reflected Tom, that MissEss had saved his bacon. As a fighting unit they were a match for all comers—him trailing a wing and taking the odd knock or two while she laid out the opposition in rows.

"Miss Seeton came to see you," continued Deirdre, "but that dragon of a ward sister wouldn't let her in, so she left some grapes and asked me to give you this." She took a bulky envelope from her handbag.

Tom put out his right hand, started to lean forward, winced, and desisted. "Wha's innit?" he inquired.

With mock solemnity, Deirdre opened the envelope and fanned out the contents on the bed. "Five hundred pounds," she announced.

"Wha'—wha'?" quacked Tom incredulously.

"Wha' indeed," she retorted. "I gather you asked her to back a horse for you—though I'd hardly've called it a horse—so she did and these are your ill-gotten gains. Apparently she tipped the parents off about it as well and Father went quite mad and stuck five hundred on it. Poor sweets. They're feeling pretty downtrodden about Derrick, but ten thousand quid's boosted their morale quite a bit. I do think"—Deirdre looked wistful—"Miss Seeton might've tipped me off too—all I did was lose fifty p. By the way, the parents came to see you, too, but the dragon wouldn't let 'em in either. They left you some grapes. Sister also barred the Forby-Banner pair, which took some doing. They—er—left grapes. And she tried to chuck me out as well until I explained . . ." Deirdre's color rose and her fingers intertwined and twisted, then she chuckled. "I'm afraid I brought some too—so between the lot of us you're rather overgraped."

Tom glanced sideways at the bed table, which sported a dish piled high with an overflowing cascade of blackish-purple and green. He looked again at the money on the coverlet. "Not mine," he said, " 'nly half—we were splittin'." Pain was increasing and he felt muddled. But there was something . . . yes. "Car park," he asked. "Wha' happened?"

"The police rounded up most of the boys," Deirdre told him. "A few got away—Derrick amongst them." She shrugged and her hands expressed doubt. "I don't know whether I'm glad or sorry."

"That's quite enough." The ward sister rustled to the bedside with a kidney-shaped bowl and an air of starched efficiency. "I've let you have five minutes more than I said." She produced a thermometer from the breast pocket of her uniform, shook it, examined it severely and thrust it into Tom's mouth, then put a finger on his pulse. She eyed with disapproval the money littering the tidy bed. "Now, we can't have this sort of thing. I told you not to excite the patient."

"But it's his—" began Deirdre. Around the thermometer Tom attempted protest, but was quelled with a glance.

"I can't help that. We don't want it here. You'd better keep it for him."

Obediently Deirdre collected the notes, stuffed them back into the envelope and replaced it in her bag. She stood up and smiled at Tom. "I'll give it back to Miss Seeton and you can settle up with her." He nodded.

The ward sister was adamant. "Now off you go." With a flutter of fingers to Tom, Deirdre took a reluctant departure. "Perhaps"—the brusqueness softened fractionally—"you can see him again tomorrow. We'll see what doctor says." The sister released Tom's wrist, removed the thermometer, frowned and clicked her tongue. "You shouldn't have had any visitors at all." She took a hypodermic from the bowl, held it up while she slightly depressed the plunger to remove air, swabbed his arm and jabbed in the needle with swift, painless efficiency. "But your fiancée was so upset and insistent that I thought . . ."

Her thoughts failed to impinge on Tom. One word stood out to loom and fill his mind. His fiancée? His fian . . . ? His fi . . . ? The plunger went home. Bars of light flickered across Tom's vision, the ward tilted forward, turned over. His fian . . . ? Hish fi . . . ? The ward sister's face in close-up back-somersaulted twice. The screen went blank.

chapter

~10~

DUTIFULLY MISS SEETON watched the television screen in the saloon bar, which reenacted for her the grandstand, the crowds, the horses at the race meeting which she had attended less than three hours since, while the commentator described the teen-age riot which had taken place. It was extraordinary, she reflected, when you came to think of it, how quickly news was disseminated nowadays, even though so many other things were slower. Like travel or the post. Naturally one could understand Mel and Mr. Banner wishing to catch up, as they called it, on the news, since news was their livelihood, but to stop at this roadhouse, near Wrotham—how very odd that it should be pronounced Rootem—when they were so near home—less than thirty miles, she thought—had been, she must admit, a little disappointing. And then again, orangeade—she drank some more and put the glass down upon the round tabletop— though very kind, was not quite the same as tea.

"The police wish to interview Derrick Ken- harding . . ."

The name recalled Miss Seeton's wandering attention.
That poor family. And she still felt guilty that she had been,
at least in part, responsible for the latest trouble with their
son. Yet while she was trying to apologize when saying
good-bye, Lord Kenharding had shaken her most warmly
by the hand and Lady Kenharding had suddenly hugged her,
kissed her on the cheek and actually thanked her—though
for what Miss Seeton could not imagine.

". . . *get in touch with their local police.*" A photograph of Derrick was faded out and another face was
substituted.

To Miss Seeton's trained eye, the absence of a checked
cap and raincoat was not bar to recognition. Oh, good
gracious. That reminded her. She'd forgotten to remember.
She burrowed in her handbag.

"What's biting you, Miss S.?" asked Mel. "Want a
tissue?"

"It's that man," explained Miss Seeton, indicating the
television screen. "You see, I'd meant to ask Deirdre, or
give it to Tom—Mr. Haley—but with all that happened
afterwards I'm afraid it completely slipped my mind."

". . . *remembers seeing this man or noticed anything
unusual in the paddock before the third race should inform
the Guildford police*"—the figure of a telephone number
appeared below Fingers' face—"*or contact their local
force.*"

"What?" asked Thrudd.

"What?" echoed Miss Seeton.

"This mental skid of yours—what was it?"

"I don't know," she confessed. "That is to say, it looked
rather like a large . . ." She shook her head and appealed
to Mel. "But then it couldn't have been, because he
wouldn't use one, would he?"

"Wouldn't," said Mel patiently, "use what?"

"A powder compact."

"Improbable," Thrudd acknowledged. Miss Seeton's
burrowing had evidently proved fruitful, and realizing this
from her expression, he leaned quickly across, took the
handbag, made a show of searching in his turn, gave her a

handkerchief, returned the bag and let his hand, with the palm gum concealed in it, drop beneath the tabletop.

Mel watched with interest. "Bag snatching yet," she observed.

Thrudd was engrossed with his find. He aimed the nozzle at the floor, depressed the plunger and was rewarded with a click, felt rather than heard. For dope, he'd guess. Yeah, some form of dope gun or he was a Tibetan yak. "Where'd you get it?" he inquired.

Miss Seeton gave her own somewhat involved version of the circumstances. ". . . and I picked it up when he dropped it and ran away," she concluded. Looking up, she saw that the photograph of Fingers was gone and the news had passed on to banal trivialities, with the commentator describing a debate in the House upon in- and deflation.

Thrudd was skeptical. All very innocent-sounding—as usual—and, even allowing for her earnest endeavors to make things clear, which invariably made them anything but, all very pat. But he'd lay odds this man Fingers had been her assignment, that she'd picked his pocket for the evidence, meaning to follow it up, but the fight had prevented her. And could be—just could be—it was true she'd forgotten it till now. Anyway, the cops were clamoring for information, so they'd better have it pronto, which, he realized with satisfaction, would help to solve his own immediate problem.

As though divining the trend of his thoughts, Mel remarked, "You didn't like the Humber either."

"No," he agreed, remembering his unexpressed anxiety during the drive from Guildford. "I didn't like the Humber either."

Mel lifted an eyebrow. "And that's why we're stuck in this pub?"

"And that's why we're stuck in this pub. Could be I'm wrong—I'm not," he asserted, "but just could be—that they didn't try to run us off the road twice and we happened to be plain lucky with the traffic and winding roads. But"— he visualized the road that still lay ahead of them—"just beyond here we turn left onto the Dover motorway for a

stretch. Wide, straightish and not so crowded." He gave a
short laugh. "It'd be a gift for 'em. Against a Humber, my
old flivver wouldn't have time for so much as a short
prayer."

"So," Mel asked, "we stay put till we think they're well
clear?"

"Hardly," replied Thrudd dryly. "The Humber's now
sitting in the car park and I've been trying to work out how
to tell the local cops I think we're being followed without
sounding like a hopeful virgin."

Mel gave him a sideways glance. "Hopeful, maybe—
virgin, no."

"Which makes this here"—under cover of the table he
slipped the palm gun into his pocket—"the answer to my
maiden's prayer. The police want info—right, they can
come and get it. Who," he asked Miss Seeton, who had
been trying unsuccessfully to follow the exchange, "do you
know among the local constabulary?"

She considered. "Well, there's Mr. Potter, of course,
who lives in the village, but I'm afraid," she apologized,
"he's not always there since he's had a car to make him
what they call mobile." She frowned. "The only other one I
really know is Chief Inspec—no, I believe he's now Chief
Superintendent Brinton at Ashford."

"Made to measure," exclaimed Thrudd with delight.
"I'm all for highly polished brass." He jumped to his feet,
adjusted his camera strap and collected the glases. "I'll get
us another round, slope off to the gents', take a couple of
shots of MissEss' little toy, phone the office to hold for a
follow-up on the racecourse story, then get on to this
Brinton character, filling him in and asking for an escort."

"You don't think," suggested Mel, "that Miss S., as she
knows Brinton, might get quicker action than your invisible
boyish charm?"

Thrudd looked at her. "I like people to be happy," he
explained kindly. "You and MissEss are happy sitting here
boozing and watching the world go by, and one of the lads
from the Humber—third stool from the left at the end of
the bar," he elaborated, noting Mel's involuntary glance

around, "is happy watching you and MissEss watching the world et cetera. If I set up another round"—he eased past the table—"my call of nature shouldn't disturb his happiness and with any luck he won't cotton that I'm calling the law."

Thrudd Banner's call was received with a marked lack of enthusiasm by the law in the person of Chief Superintendent Brinton.

"So all right, you're at Wrotham; so it's Maidstone's pigeon. Give 'em a ring 'nd maybe they'll get a squad car to keep an eye on you. Why get on to me?"

Thrudd began to amplify that Miss Seeton— He heard a choking sound, then silence. "Hello . . . hello," said Thrudd.

"Shuddup," said Brinton. Miss Seeton. Hell and damnation. That meant this particular pigeon was coming home to roost—in his bailiwick. He repressed a groan. If she was on the rampage again they'd likely need a fleet of cars, air cover—the lot. "Why'n't did you say Miss Seeton to start with?" he snapped. "So all right, let's have it from the beginning."

Thrudd gave him a synopsis of the afternoon's events. It was received with a gusty sigh. "Humph. She goes to the races, goes to war and's now all set to stage the next battle on her home ground. That makes my day. What's this gadget you say she's got hold of?" Thrudd told him his guess. "A squirter for dope? She tried it on anybody yet?" Brinton's tone was caustic. "Well, don't give it back or she will. You can hand it over to . . . No, you can't. Wait." Brinton had been jolted by a memory of Miss Seeton being abducted by a sham police officer, resulting in a fire which had destroyed a wood, a church, the abductor and very nearly Miss Seeton herself. He grimaced; they could do without another cock-up of that sort.

"So all right," he said at length. "I've got a D.C. here who wears fancy dress and calls it, God forgive him, plain clothes; name of Foxon. He knows her, and she him. I'll have him ferried over to you—'bout half an hour. Got room

for him in your bus? . . . Good. Give the doohickey to
him, take fancypants with you and I'll have him picked up
in Plummergen later. But be damn sure," he emphasized,
"that it is Foxon and that she does know him. I'll ask
Maidstone to keep an eye on the Humber—got its registration? . . . Right. And yours?" He jotted the numbers
down and rang off.

Could be all my eye, Brinton decided, but better warn
Maidstone there might be trouble. If there'd been all this
shenanigans at the races and if this reporter fellow was right
that there'd been a couple of tries to run 'em off the road,
the villains weren't going to pack it in just because
somebody wagged a finger at them and said tut. Calamitous
experience had taught him, where Miss Seeton was concerned, to expect the worst, then double it and add the date.
How that butter-wouldn't-melt-in-the-mouth little schoolmarm managed to stir up more hornets' nests in five minutes
than ten normal people could in a lifetime . . . ? Brinton
sighed again, sent for Foxon and picked up the receiver.

The hair was on the long side, the pants, in a startling
shade of terra cotta, clashed with the brightly striped and
pleated shirt, from the neckband of which streamed a tie of
many colors. The young man put his hands on Miss
Seeton's shoulders and with a mixture of deference and
affection bent and kissed her on the cheek. Miss Seeton
looked startled.

Thrudd Banner's eyes narrowed. "You do know this
character?"

"Mr. Foxon?" Miss Seeton smiled. "Good gracious,
yes. We spent a night together." Thrudd's expression made
her realize that she had not, perhaps, been sufficiently
explicit. She hastened to make it clear. "It was all most
peculiar," she elaborated. "And then, of course, being in a
church seemed, somehow, to make it even more. Peculiar, I
mean."

"Original anyway," observed Mel.

Thrudd took his hand from his pockets and shook hands

with the newcomer. Foxon palmed the dope gun without a flicker of surprise while Thrudd introduced him to Mel.

Foxon grinned. "I saw Miss Forby once in action during a punch-up at Plummergen. She wields a wicked handbag."

Memory stirred details of her first assignment to Miss Seeton's affairs. "You," said Mel, "were the one who finished the scrap wearing a tie and little else."

"Reunion of veterans in the MissEss army," commented Thrudd. "We'll have a final round on that, for the benefit of our pal from the Humber at the bar, then we'll get weaving."

Foxon fetched the drinks in order to obtain a closer view of their adversary. "You were all in this afternoon's do that was on the news?" he asked on his return.

"In," admitted Mel, "and only just out. Miss S.'s pet policeman had to be sewn together and dumped in hospital, but at least"—with satisfaction—"more than half the yobs were collared by the law."

"And what's the betting"—Foxon looked sour—"they'll get a lawyer to swear 'they never' and were only barging in to help?"

"Won't wash for some of 'em," Thrudd assured him. "I got in a couple of shots before they rushed us, including one of the character who was waving a gun and did a quick fade-out when the action started."

Foxon leaned forward. He and Mel spoke together: "You've got . . . ?"

Thrudd shook his head. "Not with me. Put the film on a train to London, collect, when you"—he eyed Mel with sad reproof—"were being reshod. Told you if you stuck around with me you'd begin to learn the elements of your job. Come on." He rose. "We'd best be on our way while the Humber and the cops play cops and robbers."

A patrol car was drawn up blocking the Humber when Thrudd drove out onto the main road.

Two police officers had approached on either side of their objective. "Excuse me, sir, but this is not a public car park. I'm afraid you can't wait here unless you're having a meal or a drink."

The man at the wheel of the Humber let out a breath of relief. "Me friend's inside knockin' back a couple," he explained. "Me, I never drink when 'm drivin'," he added virtuously.

"Very wise, sir." The policeman remained wooden-faced and held out his hand. "May I see your driving license and insurance certificate? Just a matter of routine," he appended as the other was about to protest.

For an instant it appeared that the driver was going to refuse, then his gaze flicked past his interrogator, he gave a short laugh and put his hand in his breast pocket. "Anything t' oblige."

There was the sound of a thwack and the police officer collapsed. With an exclamation, his teammate swung round, but the man from the bar had already launched himself across the hood and, with the advantage of surprise, caught his opponent off balance and brought him down, while the driver, who had slid across the seat to the passenger door, fell on him, pinioning him and knocking off his cap. The man from the bar brought his sap down hard on the exposed base of the skull and the patrolman lay still.

The whole episode had taken less than a minute and, screened by the cars ranged on either side and the police car in front, had passed unnoticed. The two men wasted neither time nor speech. It was evident, or likely, that the registration of their car had been reported. Without a word they stripped the jackets from the police officers, took their caps, bundled the unconscious forms into the back of the Humber, donned their borrowed plumes, of which the ill fit would be unremarkable to the world outside, threw their own coats on the rear seat of the patrol car, found the key still in the ignition, switched on, swept out of the car park and headed for the motorway in pursuit of Miss Seeton and the strong probability that she was still in possession of the palm gun, since the man with the pistol had seen her collect something from the grass in the paddock and drop it into her handbag after Fingers' flight.

Miss Seeton was beginning to feel tired. She had not, she feared, altogether accepted Mr. Foxon's reason for joining them. That he was glad to "cadge a lift" to Plummergen, since he had business there and where he could easily get another lift back to Ashford, might be true, but the manner rather than the matter of his ingenuous explanation smacked strongly of a long line of spurious excuses from children in class. However, his was none of hers—business, that was to say—and it was pleasant to see him again. The unfortunate weekend at Kenharding Abbey was now behind her and soon the more infelicitous episodes would fade from her mind. Many people tend to forget or to translate experiences in their lives which do not fit with their own conception of themselves and Miss Seeton was a past mistress of this art. Already the riot in the car park was assuming something of the nature of a student demonstration. To protest was indigenous to youth, she mused. After all, if she remembered rightly, the very word "university" derived from students forming a guild to protect their rights and protest, sometimes with violence, against bad conditions in thirteenth- and fourteenth-century Europe. She nodded agreement with her thoughts. It took many years of living to accept life, to appreciate the advantages of tranquillity, and though to the young her own life would appear humdrum . . . Drum, drum? echoed the engine of the car in faint astonishment. Yes. She nodded again with satisfaction. Quite humdrum . . . Drum, drum? repeated the car. Humdrum . . . drum, drum? Humdrum . . . drum . . . drum . . . ? Miss Seeton nodded herself to sleep.

Thrudd was keeping a watchful eye on his driving mirror. No sign of the escort they'd been promised. Maybe the police car that had been blocking the Humber when they left had wrapped things up and they were considered in the clear. Now that he had passed the buck to the cops, he was beginning to realize what a strain the drive from Guildford had been from the time he'd begun to suspect the black car that appeared to be sitting on their trail, twice trying to pull alongside, only to be forced back by oncoming traffic. After that, when the road ahead had been clear, he'd kept to the crown, weaving when necessary, to forestall any attempt to pass. But yes, he could admit, it had been a bit of a strain. Among the scatter of cars behind he caught a glimpse of blue and white. It gained on them rapidly until the protruding light on the roof became visible along with the mirrored sign ƎƆI⅃Oꟼ. Thrudd expelled a sigh of relief.

Foxon was worried. The chief superintendent had bunged him over to that pub at Wrotham all in a hurry, saying to join Miss Seeton's party, making like an old friend, and see she got safely home. Fair enough. But what old Brimmers hadn't said was why. Also, no brolly. Funny. That worried him most. Miss Seeton without an umbrella seemed . . . Well, it was wrong. He'd asked if she'd forgotten it when they were leaving the pub but Miss Forby'd said no, she'd chucked it at a horse. A joke, of course, but . . . Well, Miss Seeton did do odd things. Sometimes you thought she was almost gaga until it was all over and the dust had settled, and then you'd find she'd been on the ball all the time. He looked with affection at the sleeping form beside him. Anyway, the old girl obviously thought everything was under control or she wouldn't be taking a kip. Foxon glanced out of the rear window for the eighth time. Ah. A blue and white job was coming up on them fast—roof light, the sign ƎƆI⅃Oꟼ. Good. Maidstone was doing its stuff. Foxon relaxed.

The blue and white Panda pulled out and drew alongside. The uniformed man in the passenger seat pointed to a lay-by some hundred yards ahead, then the car went ahead, blinked its left indicator light, crossed their path, slowed and entered the lay-by. Obediently Thrudd eased his foot on the accelerator, flipped his indicator lever in turn and prepared to follow.

Foxon leaned forward and spoke urgently. "Don't track 'em. Carry on—and go like hell." Instinctively he had lowered his voice because Miss Seeton slept.

"Sure." Thrudd swerved back onto the motorway and put his foot down hard. "Why?" he asked mildly.

"They're phony." The policeman sounded incredulous. "The one who signaled us was that chap in the bar at the pub."

"Oh." Thrudd expressed resignation. "In that case we haven't a prayer. This poor old thing"—he patted the steering wheel—"might manage sixty-eight downhill with the wind up her exhaust, but it'd probably shake her apart at the seams."

From beside Thrudd Mel looked back, and noticing that Miss Seeton slept, she also kept her voice down. "They're after us. But"—her speech quickened with excitement—"we *have* a prayer—two, in fact. Our tail's got two tails."

Foxon turned to scan the road behind. The Panda, darting from the lay-by, was already a bare twenty yards behind, but behind *it* a couple of flashing blue lights were racing down the fast lane. Maidstone to the rescue. The chief inspector must have put them well in the picture. Trust old Brimmers. Foxon could see the cars clearly now—a couple of black Wolseleys. That meant probably eight men. Foxon relaxed and prepared to enjoy the chase, thankful that with only light traffic on the road, they weren't using their sirens, since Miss Seeton slept.

The men in the Panda, now abreast and trying to force Thrudd over toward the left shoulder, must at that point have noticed their pursuers, for the car abruptly straightened course and shot ahead. Foxon chuckled to himself. The Wolseleys'd have the wheels on them. A moment later, Thrudd still holding grimly to the center lane, the two black police cars streaked by on either side, the occupants giving encouraging "V" salutes as they passed. An elderly gentleman, wearing his head and hat rigidly erect, who was traveling at a steady thirty-five miles per hour down the fast lane, became furious, then flustered, as one police car after another gave warning hoots before cutting by on his inside. He lost his nerve, his control, mounted the grass and ground to a surprised halt against the central crash barrier, thus clearing the road in front to provide Mel, Thrudd and Foxon with an uninterrupted, if distant, view of the hunt.

The Panda veered from one side of the road to the other to avoid being overtaken, but the two police cars behind fanned out and awaited their chance to catch it in a scissors movement. First one, then the other, drew slightly ahead and the drivers turned their wheels toward each other. The Panda's driver, realizing that if he braked so would his opponents, took the only course left to him. He stamped on the accelerator in an attempt to escape the closing jaws of the pincers, but the police held their positions, narrowing the gap, and the Panda hit the fenders of both Wolseleys, bringing all three cars to a standstill with a metallic rending shriek.

Other vehicles pulled up to enjoy the spectacle, but were waved on their way, and when Thrudd, arriving at a sedate pace, slowed, he too was waved forward by a grinning officer. The two reporters and Foxon waved acknowledgment and gave a thumbs-up sign, but forebore to cheer in consideration of the fact that Miss Seeton slept.

"Three flippin' cars she's churned up. Maidstone's wild." Chief Superintendent Brinton gripped the telephone receiver tighter for emphasis. "Can't you control her, Oracle? So all right the Yard hoicks her off to London an' she gets in a fight. So all right you send her to Kempton, where she starts a war. All right by me, but can't you keep her away from us until the flippin' war's over?"

"Hardly." Delphick gazed blankly across his office in Scotland Yard, envisaging his empurpled old friend down at Ashford under threat of Miss Seeton's return to his district, trailing the afterclap of her latest gambade behind her. "She does live in Plummergen," he affirmed mildly, "and I can hardly forbid her to go home."

"Then for God's sake," urged Brinton, "send someone down to keep tabs on her. You know her shenanigans are way out of our class. She'll run the whole force off their feet and all the cars off the road and we can't cope. What about that young giant of a sergeant of yours? After all, he's half local since he married the doctor's daughter."

"I might." Delphick's mouth twisted ironically. "In fact, could be I'm involved already. A casino called The Gold Fish, where all this started, was burnt down last night—or rather early this morning. They've found the remains of a time fuse, which makes it crime, and also the remains of the proprietor, which brings in Homicide. According to his secretary, the owner seemed worried and said he'd be spending the night in his office to keep an eye on the place. I doubt they meant to kill him, or even knew he was there—but it's still murder."

"Hmph." Brinton was sobered. "A toe-the-line-or-else which went too far." He waxed indignant again. "And that's the place where you had the gall to send your girl friend."

"Not I," Delphick corrected him. "Fraud."

"Well, it was you," insisted Brinton, "who brought her back. I heard through our local man Potter, whose wife keeps her ear to the ground, that a whole party of you arrived in the middle of the night in front of the whole village, as tight as ticks and with her all dolled up like a tart. That's fairly put the pigeon amongst the cats. I'm told two of the local tabbies are getting up a petition she must go."

"She must go," said Miss Erica Nuttel.

"You know, I'm afraid Eric's too right," agreed Mrs. Norah Blaine—Bunny to her friend. "I do try to make allowances and think the best of people, but—"

"It's clear," pursued Miss Nuttel, "she must go."

The two ladies were known in Plummergen unaffectionately as the Nuts and their main purpose in life, useful in days of newspaper delivery strikes, was the spreading of local news, for which purpose the house they shared in the center of the village was ideally situated. From their sitting room window they could note, annotate and misinterpret almost every move made by the villagers and they were green-fingered at sowing seeds of dissension and misunderstanding in fertile soil. Their present call at Rhytham Hall, the home of Sir George and Lady Colveden, was in pursuit of their vocation. The fact that it happened to be tea-time was, naturally, fortuitous. No, really, they hadn't meant . . . They didn't want to be a trouble. . . . Well, since it was there, they wouldn't say no to a cup.

Unwillingly Lady Colveden had provided extra cups and

offered cake. The true reason the ladies had called at teatime
was in order to be sure of catching Sir George.

"Why?" asked Sir George.

Mrs. Blaine put down her plate and leaned forward to add
weight to her words. "Well, in your position as a—"

"Magistrate," supplied Miss Nuttel.

"You would know who to speak to and could use
your—"

"Influence," contributed her friend.

"Poppycock," said Sir George.

Lady Colveden broke in hurriedly. "What George means
is that I'm afraid we don't agree with you in the least.
Personally we like Miss Seeton. We think she's an asset to
the village."

"She'd be an asset anywhere," subscribed her son Nigel.

"And in any case," continued his mother, "there's
nothing you can do. This idea of a petition's ridiculous—I
mean you can't order people to go and live somewhere else
just because you don't approve of them. If you could, we
should all be moving around, like musical chairs." This
was idiotic. George and Nigel were both obviously spoiling
for a fight. Somehow she must avoid open warfare. It was
all very well for the men. But they forgot that being in a
small village, and on committees and things, any awkward-
nesses were—awkward. Firmness and tact, that was the
answer. "It's all nonsense." Firmness. "I'm sure the whole
thing is just a misunderstanding."

"Lack of understanding," corrected Nigel.

Well, it would have been tact if Nigel hadn't butted in.
Lady Colveden tried again. "What on earth's Miss Seeton
done to upset you?"

"Done?" exclaimed Norah Blaine. "You were there—
you saw her. Coming back, at that hour, in front of
everybody, dressed up like a—a—"

"Streetwalker," furnished Miss Nuttel.

"And all those men." Mrs. Blaine crumbled cake in
agitation. "And all drunk, and all that—that—"

"Money," said Miss Nuttel.

"Naturally, it's no business of ours—"

"Quite."

"Exactly," chorused father and son.

"But we do feel—"

"Strongly—" urged her friend.

"It's got to be stopped."

"Which?" asked Nigel. "The men, the drink or the money?"

"Nigel," requested Lady Colveden. "Go and boil some more hot water, would you?" She sighed with relief as her son left the room. That was one of them out of the fight for a moment.

"Oh, it's not us," insisted Mrs. Blaine. "Eric and I can look after ourselves. It's—"

"The village," stated Miss Nuttel.

"Yes, it's the effect on the village. That woman's done nothing but cause trouble ever since she's been here." Mrs. Blaine spurred her high horse to a gallop. "It's too much. We've had drugs and murder and robberies and witchcraft and the newspapers and murder and going abroad—too unsuitable at her age—and murder and television and they never"—a genuine grievance—"even used the interview I gave them and—and—"

"Prostitution," offered Miss Nuttel.

"That's what I mean. It's all too, too dreadful and that's why"—Mrs. Blaine offered Sir George a sheet of paper— "we've got up this petition and thought if you'd sign it and—"

"I?" Sir George rose, took the paper and scanned the five signatures. "Norah Lindly?" he barked. "Never heard of her. Who's she?"

"It's my maiden name," confessed Mrs. Blaine.

"You can't," he exploded, "sign a petition twice."

"Why not?" demanded Mrs. Blaine. "If you feel too strongly, as I do, and in my view—"

Miss Nuttel came to the aid of her friend. "In both our views . . ."

Sir George's plump figure appeared to swell to alarming proportions; the bristles of his military mustache became a bunch of steel needles aimed at the intruders. On the point

of stating some views of his own, he caught the appeal in
his wife's eye. He took a deep breath. Sooner he got out of
the room the better. Meg'd been right to get rid of the boy.
Smooth things over. Didn't do to lose your temper. Flattered
himself he'd kept his pretty well. But any more from these
two harpies and he'd give 'em a dressing. Best retreat now,
in good order, for Meg's sake. He threw rather than handed
back the offending paper and marched to the door. Before
he reached it, it opened to reveal Nigel, kettle in hand.
Father and son looked at each other and Sir George's good
resolutions evaporated. He turned on their visitors.

"Reminded me I'm a magistrate. Like to remind you—
both of you: any more libelous bal—" he caught the word in
midbreath: ladies present—"balderdash about friends of
ours and you'll find yourselves in—"

"Hot water?" suggested Nigel, holding out the kettle.

No one could say she hadn't tried. But her son's parody of
Miss Nuttel undid her. Lady Colveden laughed.

chapter
~11~

MISS SEETON AWOKE. She listened to the verbal sparring of the two reporters on the front seat with satisfaction. Teasing each other—such a good sign. Thank heaven, after all that had happened earlier on, this journey home had been uneventful. And . . . A sign at the roadside diverted her thoughts.

She recognized the circular metal advertisement which turned in the wind. Why, that was Mr. Hyder's garage. They

were nearly home. Yet another sign on her left—a board
with black lettering on electric orange—confirmed this.

```
PLUMMERGEN

    + +

   FETE

 - + - + - + - + -
 - + - + - + - + -
 - + - + - + - + -
 - + - + - + - + -
 - + - + - + - + -
```

And the date in three days' time. Oh, dear. She'd almost
forgotten. She'd promised Sir George, as editor, and also
Miss Treeves, the vicar's sister, to do some pen sketches of
the fête for the parish magazine. Well, she'd do her best.
Meanwhile, the relief of being nearly home again . . . a
pot of tea and the comfort of sinking into the anonymity of
village life, where no one knew, or was interested in, what
one did . . . Really, one was so very fortunate. To live a
quiet existence amid peaceful surroundings. And then
again, to have the retaining fee from Scotland Yard—for an
instant the quiet and the peace frayed slightly at the edges—
which solved her financial worries. If only, she wished, the
fête weren't quite so soon. After the rush of events during
the last few days, she would have preferred to have had just
a little more time.

For Thatcher, the timing was convenient. The only
inconvenience in his estimation had been the death of the
proprietor of The Gold Fish, which had made the police
probe more deeply into the fire than otherwise they would
have done. On the credit side, the fire and the death had
proved a salutary lesson to others. In common with all
dictators, the one thing that Thatcher could not afford was
any successful opposition, and for that the elimination of
Miss Seeton, whose continuing immortality was threatening
to make him into a laughingstock, was now essential.
The Kenharding boy, from being an asset, had become a

liability. This puny fête in the woman's tin-pot village would solve both problems in one. Send Derrick down there, backed by some of his teen-age pals, with orders to kill, and if the police didn't pick him up afterward the boy would then be on the run in earnest, without a sanctuary.

With regard to the girl, Deirdre, he had a man keeping tabs on her, waiting the opportunity for a snatch. Thatcher smiled briefly. That'd keep the father and mother in order. So far the girl had remained at Kenharding Abbey, with excursions only to the hospital at Guildford to see some foot detective constable who'd mixed himself into the affray. However, he had information that the D.C. was due to be discharged. Deirdre would come south and the rest would be easy.

Incidentally, the Plummergen fête, though small beer, would give the syndicate a chance to show they meant business in this as in all other fields of gambling. Thatcher smiled again, dismissed Miss Seeton along with the Kenhardings from his mind, and turned to more important matters.

The fête at Plummergen was in full swing. Miss Seeton had visited the marquee, in which floral arrangements, fruit and vegetables were on display, and had dutifully made one or two sketches, although she had hardly felt that the exhibits were worthy of record. She had watched the crowning of Miss Plummergen to an underrehearsed accompaniment by the village band and had made notes; though here again she had considered it was an incident better omitted, since Emmy Putts, who served behind the grocery counter at the post office, had short dark hair, and a diaphanous dress crossed by a sash emblazoned with her sovereignty did not, in Miss Seeton's opinion, counterbalance the dishonesty of a long blond wig. Also, Deirdre's scathing comments, though amusing, had not been helpful.

Miss Seeton had been taken by surprise when Deirdre Kenharding, glowing with happiness, had arrived at two o'clock, just when she herself had been prepared to set off for the fête. Tom Haley, it appeared, at his own insistence,

had been allowed to leave the hospital on the weekend and
Deirdre had given him a lift, dropping him off in London,
having arranged to meet him again that evening at The
10/20. The 10/20 had been recommended by Mel Forby as
her favorite nightclub. They would meet there, Tom had
decreed, at ten-twenty for luck, to spend a part of his
winnings, and Deirdre had then continued the journey to
Plummergen in order to bring the £250 which Tom—quite
wrongly, Miss Seeton insisted—declared that he owed her.
Deirdre, however, on Tom's behalf, was adamant and the
older woman had been forced to accept the money. Learning
of the afternoon's festivities, the girl had decided to join the
merry-go-round and was now doing so literally, rising and
sinking astride a painted wooden horse.

   Now, here, Miss Seeton looked up at a circular tower
entitled Penny-on-the-Mat. A misnomer, she decided, since
a smaller notice informed the public that it was "5p. a go."
That would be ideal. From the top she could get an overall
impression of the festival far better than she could do from
the ground. Miss Seeton paid her five pence, climbed the
steep and twisting stairway, then, balancing her sketchbook
on the wooden barrier, to one side of where people might
wish to slide on mats to their enjoyment, she settled down to
work. From this point of vantage the mass of people moving
down the lines between the gaily striped awnings resembled
ants marching in formation through the spilled contents of a
box of licorice allsorts, which had been so popular with her
pupils at the school. A fine study; a most interesting
perspective.
   A grubby youth paused alongside her.
   "Ain't cher goin' darn?" he demanded.
   "No," Miss Seeton explained. "You see, I—"
   "Y'are, y'know." He lurched, knocking Miss Seeton to
the floor and her sketchbook over the balustrade. He
reached for her. They'd never prove a broken neck wasn't
but an accident.
   Miss Seeton, to save herself, tried to hook her second-
best umbrella round the post which held the stairs. Instead

she ensnared the young man's ankle and he, off balance, uttering an expletive, flung himself against the barrier, but his victim's gathering momentum pulled his feet from under him and, still entangled with the umbrella, he described an ungraceful somersault to take the quickest route, while Miss Seeton, without benefit of mat, up one side, down the other, of the enclosing polished walls, spiraled her way to earth.

Sergeant Ranger stood transfixed. A sketchbook fluttered, a body plummeted and an umbrella arrowed down within feet of him. He stared at the Penny-on-the-Mat. He glimpsed a pair of sensible shoes; a hat—there could not be two like it; the shoes again, gray stockings showing; the hat, more crumpled than before. He ran to the end of the chute, to find Miss Seeton sitting up in dazed bewilderment.

"A young man knocked into me and I'm afraid I slipped," she explained. She looked about her. "Oh, dear. My drawing block and—"

"All present and correct." Chief Superintendent Delphick handed her her sketchbook, pencil and umbrella as he helped her to her feet.

"Oh, thank you, Chief Superintendent." Miss Seeton was relieved. "But the young man . . . ?" She looked toward the top of the tower.

"Not to worry," Delphick assured her. "He came down another way." He glanced at his sergeant. "Fell on his head, broke his neck and good riddance," he muttered. "Get her away from here while I sort things out."

The excited crowd around the "accident" prevented Miss Seeton from realizing what had happened as Bob Ranger led her to another part of the field.

Chief Superintendent Delphick had been warned by an informer that the syndicate was planning to cause trouble at the Plummergen fête. After a telephone conversation with Brinton at Ashford, he had agreed to come down himself and join his sergeant, who was already on the spot, while Brinton had pledged to infiltrate as many plainsclothesmen as he could spare. Tom Haley had reported at the Yard before Delphick's departure. Although officially on sick leave, when he had learned of possible trouble at Plummergen he begged, knowing that Deirdre was liable to arrive in the midst of it, that he should be allowed to accompany the Oracle, declaring that otherwise he'd "go it alone." Delphick agreed and also yielded to Tom's insistence, backed by his experience at Kempton, that on this occasion he should be armed. Thus, with already more than the normal complement of uniformed officers to direct the traffic, the police were present at the fête in force, but even this, Delphick was obliged to admit, had failed to prevent an attempt on Miss Seeton's life. He supervised the removal of the grubby youth's carcass by ambulance and went in search of his sergeant and Miss Seeton.

Blue—white—red—green. Miss Seeton noted the colors on her penciled sketch. If only it would keep still. If only, too, that organ were not quite so loud. The carrousel began to slacken speed and she recognized Deirdre traveling in slowing circles. Miss Seeton's pencil moved faster—lions, cocks, giraffes, bears, ostriches and horses. What a variety of animals these machines had nowadays. The difficulty, the age-old difficulty, was to convey the sense of movement. Those few artists who had achieved this had done so not by some technical trick but through a genius born into their fingers which defied analysis. Miss Seeton sighed. Painstaking she was, accurate she might be, but genius—no, she lacked it.

Miss Seeton was introducing Bob Ranger to Deirdre when she stopped in midsentence.

That tiny tot now, straining to climb up onto the platform. She opened her pad once more; her pencil flew. On her sketch quickly appeared the small, square, determined form reaching vainly upward. Here was her answer—her subject. No need to worry further over movement. It became essential for her purpose that the merry-go-round be still. That urchin should epitomize the whole human race in its everlasting and futile struggle to grasp what lay beyond its reach.

Before Deirdre or Bob had time to realize her intent, Miss Seeton had slipped her sketchbook and pencil into her handbag, moved forward, picked up the little girl, still futilely struggling, and, mounting the platform, placed her on the back of a giraffe. The child regarded her solemnly.

"Ta," said the whole human race.

Slowly the platform began to move. The organ wheezed huskily off key.

Miss Seeton looked round. "One moment please," she called. "I'm getting off."

She reached a foot down, then drew back. No, really, the ground was beginning to go by too fast. The pace quickened.

"Stop, stop," she cried.

The organ, gaining courage as it neared its key, began to blare, drowning her protests. Miss Seeton started to run. By her rushed faces, laughing mouths and waving arms. To save herself from being whirled into space, she clasped a wooden horse about its neck. Inspired by devilry, the horse rose in the air: Miss Seeton stood on tiptoe. Foiled, the horse plunged: Miss Seeton bent her knees. Gripping its bridle with one hand, she succeeded in hooking the handle of her umbrella round the brass pipe to which the beast was fixed. To waving hats, to laughter and to cries of "Atta girl" and "Ride 'em, cowboy," Miss Seeton jumped. Drat it, she'd missed. Now was her chance—now, quick. She sprang and, midst cheers that almost drowned the strident music, somewhat flustered but secure, Miss Seeton rode the whirlwind in the saddle.

"Really, it's too dreadful the way that woman behaves," declared Mrs. Blaine. "At her age too. It's too, too—"

"Vulgar," conceded Miss Nuttel.

The ladies sniffed in self-righteous unison and made their way to the tent set up for tea and scandal.

"You watch this side, I'll watch the other." Bob Ranger hurried round to the opposite flank of the calliope.

Deirdre, weak from laughter, failed to notice the group of somber, slit-eyed youths who gathered near her. The music slowed, the machine stopped and Miss Seeton alighted

almost opposite Deirdre. Amid a crowd of parents and
children dismounting, mounting or remounting, the woman
and the girl were jostled away until they reached the rifle
range. Here they were halted by a number of young men
surrounding them. A gray-haired gentleman was being
rewarded for his prowess with a blond doll which wailed
Mama when doubled over. *Crack*—a louder sound—and
Derrick Kenharding reloaded, turned and aimed a shotgun
at Miss Seeton's head.

Tom Haley, prescience and experience having guided him
to the danger spot, had little time. Deirdre was running
forward into the line of fire as Derrick's finger tightened on
the trigger. Tom snatched his pistol from its holster and took
a low snap shot, aiming for the hand. The bullet grazed
Derrick's fingers and then smashed through his jaw. The
shotgun clattered and the boy fell. The youths encircling
them quickly dispersed while Tom, aghast, stood desolate.

Deirdre, stricken, knelt, cradling the bloodstained head.
Her voice was hoarse. "You didn't—you didn't have
to . . ."

"I did," he claimed. "What else could I do? You and
MissEss were both . . . Oh, hell—what could I do?"

Miss Seeton tried to intervene but the young people were
enclosed in a world of their own.

Deirdre lowered her brother to the ground and stood, her
face stony. "This finishes"—she swallowed—"finishes
us."

Unreason begat temper. "Rubbish," he declared. "I'll
have to stay here now to order an ambulance, explain and
help clear up. I'll see you at The 10/20 tonight and we'll
talk things over then."

Her jaw set. "No. We can't . . ." She faltered, then
was obdurate. "We can't meet again."

"I'll see you," he ordered, "at The 10/20." He holstered
his pistol and held out a hand in appeal. She ignored it.
He dropped his hand and turned away. "If not, then it
doesn't matter"—his voice hardened—"never did. We're
through."

•   •   •

Deirdre and Miss Seeton repaired to the latter's cottage, where the urgent business of cleaning the bloodstains from the girl's clothes had left Miss Seeton no time to remove her own outer garments.

A uniformed P.C. borrowed from the fête was on duty by the front gate, more to protect them from curiosity than from danger, since the story was being broadcast, lightly buttered with fact and heavily spread with the jam of fiction by Miss Nuttel and Mrs. Blaine, that Miss Seeton had deliberately shot a young man at the festival and was now under house arrest. Foxon, from Ashford, had requested permission to station himself inside Miss Seeton's cottage, but had been overruled by his superiors, as Delphick felt that any immediate risk was over for the moment and the police needed all the men they could muster to collect the youths involved, in the hope that Detective Constable Haley might be able to identify any of those who had taken part in the attack at Kempton.

The situation was ideal for Deirdre's shadow. After reconnoitering and finding the village practically deserted for the festivities, he told his driver to park the car by the side door to the garden, out of sight of the guard in front, while he himself slipped down to the canal road, climbed the low wall that bounded Miss Seeton's domain at the back, crossed the roof of a henhouse, dropped to the ground and made his way carefully to the kitchen entrance.

Deirdre was dressed and ready for departure. "You do see—you must see that Tom and I could never . . . Not now. I know it was really all Derrick's fault and that Tom didn't mean to . . . I know all that, but it doesn't alter things. Derrick would always be bound to come between us." Determined not to cry, she turned an anguished face toward the older woman. "I'm right—you do see that, don't you?"

"No," said Miss Seeton. "I do not."

Deirdre was jolted out of drama, however sincerely felt. Miss Seeton closed the flap of the writing desk in which

she had placed her sketchbook and began to unbutton her
coat as she looked at the girl standing by the fireplace,
distressed by the contrast between her happiness on arrival
and her present misery. "I should have thought," Miss
Seeton resumed briskly, "that it's simply a question of
whether you believe in law and order or you don't. You say
yourself that it was your brother's fault; Tom was merely
doing his duty. In other circumstances, I imagine, you
would consider Tom a hero, so to allow family feeling, or
failings, to influence your relationship appears to me as
grossly unfair to Tom. And to yourself." Remembering her
visit with Lord Kenharding to the picture gallery at the
manor, where the father had, in a way, she supposed,
foretold his son's self-destruction, Miss Seeton became
uncertain. "You must, of course, do what you think best.
For yourself, that is, if not for him. Tom, that is to say.
Best, I mean."

Her mentor's earlier astringency was helping Deirdre to
recover. "You mean that I must meet Tom tonight?"

Well, yes, she did. But perhaps it would be better not to
say so. Oh, dear. Miss Seeton suppressed a sigh. One did so
dislike giving advice—becoming involved in other people's
lives. Certainly Deirdre should be at The 10 O'clock—or
whatever it was—if her feelings for Tom were genuine and
not superficial, though naturally, of course, one could not
put it quite so bluntly.

"If your feelings for Tom are genuine, and not superficial—" began Miss Seeton.

"They are—oh, they are." Deirdre clasped Miss Seeton's
hands in gratitude. "You've made me see how silly I was
being. I'll be at The 10/20—"

"Not ternight cher won't."

The woman and the girl turned in shock to face the man
standing in the doorway, pistol in hand; Miss Seeton with
her hands raised in the classic pose of surrender, preparatory
to taking off her hat.

She was tired of troubles, and very tired of guns.
Dropping her arms, she moved toward the stranger. "Who

are you—what are you doing here?" she demanded. "And put that ridiculous thing away."

The man aimed at Deirdre; addressed Miss Seeton. "One more squawk or step from you and her nibs gets it."

Miss Seeton stopped. However incredulous she might be when it came to threats to herself, she could not ignore the danger to the girl.

"I've come for 'er—a snatch, an' no 'arm meant, 'less that's the way yer wannit," the gunman declared. "An' come to that, I'll take yer too." Couldn't leave the old biddy here—she'd call the cops. He'd heard the word has been out to do her. Twice or more. The boss was slipping. A right Charlie she was making out of his nibs. So best take her along; might be a bonus in it, he decided. Chuckling, he said, "That'll teach yer ter leave yer back door unlocked." He ushered them out, down the garden, took the side door key from a nail in the jamb, forced them into the back of the waiting car, sat between them, making them lie on the floor under a rug until they were out of the district, ordered the man at the wheel to back down a few yards, take the road to Plummergen Station—which, in true English rural tradition, is some two miles south of the village on the road to Romney March—branch left for Ashford and head for London.

Once clear of the vicinity and likely roadblocks, the gunman told the driver to pull up by a telephone kiosk. He handed over his pistol and put through a call to London for guidance.

On his return, he said to the driver, "We're to 'ang abaht till dark before makin' fer the smoke. Safer. Up the A-20, through Lewisham, then straight to HQ and we c'n 'and 'em over. Right, you two." He flipped back the rug. "Yer c'n sit up now if yer keeps quiet an' be'aves." Aware of the futility of protest, Miss Seeton, her hat askew, and Deirdre, her hair mussed, took their places on either side of him.

The car kept to side roads, halted near a public house while the driver fetched two hot meat pies and two cans of

Courage's pale ale. Further on, a small coppice provided a
suitable lay-by. The car was pulled off the road and the men
settled to their meal. Deirdre, thinking their captor's
attention was sufficiently distracted, eased down the door
handle and tried to make a break. She was rewarded by a
prod in the ribs from the pistol as he leaned across her and
slammed the door shut. The movement had made him drop
the remains of his pie and overturned the open can of beer
on the floor. Furious, he gave the girl a second jab, more
painful than the first, making her cry out.

It was after eight o'clock and dusk was closing in. He
gave the order to start for London, then settled back on the
seat and spared a glance for Miss Seeton. The old one was
proper cowed—and no wonder. It was a mistaken diag-
nosis, he could not understand that Miss Seeton, indifferent
to personal threat through disbelief in it, was in this instance
held by the evident menace to Deirdre, nor could he know
that two things roused Miss Seeton's equable temper,
unkindness and injustice, both were present here, and that
Miss Seeton was at last becoming angry.

chapter

~12~

DELPHICK WAS BITTER with self-reproach. He had been so sure that Miss Seeton would be safe for a few hours; that no further attack upon her was likely to be mounted on a moment's notice. Clearing up at the fête had taken time: five young men were detained on Haley's identification from Kempton of three "certains" and two "possibles." Haley, looking strained, was sent with the detainees to Ashford to make a formal charge, told to take a train to London and pursue his interrupted sick leave. Delphick and Bob Ranger finally repaired to Miss Seeton's cottage, only to find Deirdre's abandoned car parked by the gate and a P.C. guarding an empty nest from which the birds had flown. Roadblocks were set up, but with little hope since no data was available, and the chief superintendent, having ordered his sergeant to remain in Plummergen, set off for London in a savage mood, unconsoled by Brinton's solace: "If they've pinched MissEss, God help them. Your girl friend'll finish by shooting it out with 'em, crash the car and turn up fine and dandy. You'll see."

Miss Seeton saw the words emblazoned in fire against the
night sky:

TAKE COURAGE

they exhorted her.

Good gracious. She was startled. It was like the answer to
a prayer. Except that she hadn't. Only wondered what on
earth one could do to help poor Deirdre. As if the
Kenhardings hadn't enough trouble without this. The car
was halted at a set of traffic lights and ahead the clock tower
at Lewisham showed the time to be five minutes past ten.
Deirdre, whose intermittent protests during the last few
hours had been silenced by a curt "Stow it, chick," gazed at
the clock and abandoned hope. Tom's last words repeated in
her mind: "I'll see you at The 10/20. If not, then it doesn't
matter—never did. We're through." Strain is not conducive
to rational thought and for Deirdre it had become all-
important to obey this new imperative to be at the place and
at the time appointed and thus atone for her lack of empathy.
Somehow she knew that later explanations, even should she
ever have the chance and justified though they might be,
would be lame; could never have the same impact. Quite
simply, she desperately wanted Tom and despite taut self-
control an occasional tear ran down her cheek.

Since the indignity of being thrust to the floor of the car
under a rug, Miss Seeton had not uttered a word during the
seemingly endless hours. There was nothing helpful that she
could say and to argue with the man was, obviously, a waste
of time and might, she feared, make Deirdre's situation
worse, so why waste one's breath? From what the wretched
man had said, she knew that their present predicament in no
way concerned herself. She was merely there because she
was there. There at the time, that was. It was better to wait
until they met someone with more authority, when she
would, most certainly, speak her mind. Meanwhile, sympathy for the Kenharding family and her distaste for the

whole of this quite ridiculous situation had produced in her a state which some of her former pupils might have described as a "slow burn." Miss Seeton glanced across at Deirdre to give the girl reassurance, saw the telltale glint of tears, and the heat of her feelings rose to simmer.

When the traffic light changed to green at the clock tower, the car turned to the right and again, high on a building, Miss Seeton was faced with orange neon, which informed her that

COURAGE IS THE ANSWER

Of course. How foolish to have experienced a moment of superstitious qualm. This must be, she imagined, some of that modern advertising which the church used nowadays.

The car accelerated.

"Left," shouted the gunman. "Left here, you fool."

With little room to spare, the driver swung hard to the left and the car's right wheels mounted the curb of a central island, throwing its three passengers to one side.

As they righted themselves, instinctively Miss Seeton tried to straighten her much-abused hat. For a third and final time she was given the signal. Above a public house, partly obscured by buildings in front, coyly peeped the message:

KE COURAGE

Without pausing to consider action or reaction, Miss Seeton obeyed the injunction from on high, took courage and a hatpin, and with the former stuck the latter into the gunman's hand.

There was a yell of anguish, an explosion, and the bullet, passing through the driver's neck, starred the windshield. Deirdre grabbed the pistol before their captor could recover, while the car, still on its leftward gambit, careened across the traffic to an accompaniment of brake squeals, horns and imprecations, climbed the pavement amid shrieks from scattering pedestrians, detonated a plate-glass window and came to rest inside a shop.

•   •   •

Among the first to reach the scene of the smash was a
policeman on the beat. He pushed his way through the
gathering crowd and ignoring for the time being protesta-
tions, ejaculations, explanations, he stepped carefully over
shards of glass and entered the shop. The lights were blown
and the car blocked most of the illumination from the street.
At first dim glance the floor space of Chez Charlotte
appeared to be strewn with victims of the disaster as if a
child had flung down all her dolls in a fit of temper. A man
was slumped over the steering wheel of the car; the
passenger door hung open; the back seat was empty. The
form of a girl lay half under the vehicle and the officer knelt
and took a grip under the arms to lift her free. The body was
stiff and as he raised it the neck swiveled obscenely, the
long pale hair fell off, followed by the head. He jerked
upright in surprise and was left holding the arms, while the
torso dropped at his feet and bounced. He swore under his
breath: to be kidded by a plastic dummy. Taking his
personal radio, he called in.

"Bomb exploded at Cheese Charlotte," he reported.

Told to stay on the spot and to do his best for any injured
pending the arrival of an ambulance and reinforcements, he
pocketed his radio and switched on his torch. The beam
picked out a girl and a small elderly woman, both dusty and
dissheveled, sitting on a man—no, he wasn't to be fooled
again: sitting on a male model. Both women closed their
eyes against the glare. He lowered the beam, to find that the
elder of the two held a pistol in her lap aimed at his chest.
He snapped off the torch, side-stepped, stumbled over
unidentified objects, recovered, switched on again and
seized the gun from unresisting fingers.

"Thank you, officer," said Miss Seeton with relief.

"Have you got a license for this?" he demanded.

"Certainly not." She was indignant. "It's not mine. It
belongs to—" She stopped and she and Deirdre rocked on
their perch as the male model heaved beneath them and
emitted an inarticulate grunt.

The policeman was beginning to feel that he had strayed into some wonderland where he must quicken his pace in order to stand still. He took a deep breath. "Why are you sitting on him?"

"To hold him down," answered Deirdre reasonably. "What else could we do?"

She had jumped from the car as it came to a halt; the gunman had leaped after her, tripped and fallen, and with presence of mind she had sat on his head, but unable to control his thrashing, had called to Miss Seeton for help. Their combined weight had kept him pinned to the ground and Deirdre, unused to guns, had thrust the pistol into her companion's unwilling hand. They dared not move until help should arrive and the reassurance, in silhouette, of a policeman's helmet advancing toward them had, after the strain of the last few hours, made the girl almost light-headed.

"But you could smother him, miss," he objected.

"Good," retorted Deirdre.

Knowing his grasp of the situation was slipping, the officer clutched at a straw of unalterable fact. "This bomb—was it in the car or the shop?"

"Bomb?" repeated Deirdre blankly.

"Bomb?" echoed Miss Seeton.

The girl began to giggle and Miss Seeton, recognizing incipient hysteria, realized that she must explain—from the beginning. Lucidly.

"When this man"—she indicated the body below her—"did what he called a 'snatch'—after the fête, that was—" One must be clear. "That is to say, the fête was still going on. But we weren't. At it, I mean. Or not then—"

"The bomb?" He interrupted her stubbornly, clinging to his straw.

"Oh, that." Looking around her with gloom-accustomed eyes, occasional details flecked by in torchlight, she could appreciate his misapprehension. Of course. He was right. So simple, really, to explain quite briefly. "It wasn't a bomb," she assured him. "You see, I'm afraid it was me."

• • •

"She what?" ejaculated Delphick, startled. "Pins?"

Suffering from self-recrimination, the chief superintendent had remained at the Yard, tapping every source of
information he could think of without result, and now this
call from Lewisham. In his relief he glared at the telephone
receiver as though he held it responsible for Miss Seeton's
latest escapade.

"Well, if she and Miss Kenharding want to go to this club
and Miss Seeton says it's urgent, it probably is. If I were
you I'd get them there at the double." He listened for a
moment. "Surely signed statements and formal charges can
wait till later—morning, if necessary. They won't run away.
But if she's determined to go to this place she'll get there,
somehow, and if you try and stop her she'll probably stick
pins in you too." He listened again and sighed. "All right,
if it helps I'll go along to this 10/20 and be responsible for
her. What's overtime?" Humor surfaced as strain subsided,
and Delphick laughed. "I could bear, myself, to know just
what's been going on and above all find out exactly where it
was she stuck the pins."

chapter

-13-

AT THE 10/20, Tom Haley finished his drink and checked his watch for the seventh time. She wasn't coming. Well, what did he expect? Lord Kenharding's daughter—and him? That was a laugh, a right one for the birds. She'd said she wouldn't, and wasn't. And yet . . . For the sixth time he told himself he'd give it five more minutes. Not a second more. After that the hell with it—and her. So it was a pity it'd been that punk Derrick—so what? You did your job, best you could, and if people thought you'd pull your punches and risk other people's lives just because people were people, then people could stuff themselves. Again he looked at his watch. Three minutes and twenty seconds—then finish. Final. And yet . . . He clenched his teeth. Forget it.

From an alcove on the far side of the restaurant Mel Forby was keeping intermittent watch on Haley. She eyed a query as Thrudd Banner returned to the table.

"No dice," he informed her. "No answer from MissEss'

cottage. At the office the news desk says the local man from
Kent phoned in a story about trouble at some fête at
Plummergen: a man fell and broke his neck; some other
man was shot. He doesn't know who in either case—the
police've clammed up. I tried the Yard—you'd think they'd
never heard of MissEss, but were very interested in yours
truly. My name, my parents' names, date of birth of great-
auntie's Pekingese—in fact, anything to keep me on the line
while they traced the call, so I hung up.''

Mel was worried. "All of which, normally speaking,
could spell kidnap."

"Could," he agreed, "except that nothing around
MissEss is ever normal. One other thing—dunno if it
connects. The office told me a flash from Lewisham says a
bomb went off in some dress shop; a car involved; one man
removed on a stretcher, another in cuffs, and two women,
one old, one young, went off in a police car like scalded
cats, according to an eyewitness."

"A bit far-fetched—" began Mel, then stopped. The
buzz of conversation and the clink of cutlery had died.
There was a scatter of polite applause from diners anticipat-
ing a cabaret turn. Mel looked toward the entrance. "One
scalded cat?" she murmured.

The hush in the room followed by the sporadic clapping
penetrated Tom Haley's gloom. He turned and raised his
eyes, his jaw slackened and, open-mouthed, he stared at the
railed dais above the steps that led down to the dining room.
She was standing there.

She stood there. The unanchored hat hung precariously;
one half of the coat collar was up, the other down; two
jacket buttons were missing; the skirt was torn; the petticoat
showed; one grey stocking was wrinkled, the other lad-
dered; the sensible shoes were scuffed.

The headwaiter hurried forward to remove the offense. In
common with the doorman and the cloakroom attendant
before him, who had tried the same tactics, he slowed and
stopped, quelled by her regard, feeling like a schoolboy

caught out in a gaucherie. Miss Seeton was standing for no further nonsense this evening; she walked straight to Tom Haley's table and sat down.

"Deirdre's sorry to be late," she apologized. "She's in the cloakroom cleaning up. Herself, I mean."

Thrudd Banner had paid the bill. He pushed back the table.

"C'mon. Let's get the story."

"Hold it." Mel put her hand on his arm. "I'm not asking the impossible of you—like tact. I'm not suggesting you could understand what's obviously passed you by—a long way by—like Love's Young Dream. But can't even you see, you oaf, that if we butt in now they wouldn't even know we existed?"

Soon after Deirdre had arrived at the table, Miss Seeton had risen, unnoticed. She spoke to the waiter and to the wine waiter, who stood in expectation; studied the menu, glanced at the wine list, discussed, pointed; they bowed, she nodded and was now making her way toward the exit.

Mel was watching the scene. Deirdre's hands, agonized, fluttered and explained. Tom leaned across and clasped them. In a moment, the hands, the girl, relaxed and stilled. The two young people remained, hands and spirits intertwined, wondering into each other's eyes, oblivious to all else. A shadow of wistful longing sped across Mel's face.

Thrudd was watching Mel. He took her up on her last dictum.

"Young?" he drawled. "All right, let's skip young. Dream? Dreams are insubstantial things—they fade. But love . . ." His eyebrows twisted quizzically, his mouth derided. "Tell me, purely as a matter of academic interest: what would be your reaction to love?"

Under the intent gaze in the mocking face, Mel for once was speechless. For the first time since being hauled in front of a class at school to recite "Mother o' Mine," she blushed.

Thrudd sprang to his feet. "C'mon, you half-baked cub reporter—work."

As Miss Seeton reached the steps, the reporters fell in on either side of her. They spoke in unison.

"Miss S."

"MissEss."

"Give."

Miss Seeton stopped in momentary astonishment, then, accepting their unheralded appearance, "I thought they would need food," she explained, "and I was afraid that they might forget. To order, that is. So I told the one man to bring a light wine." She looked worried. "Was that all right, do you think? And I asked the other one to choose something nourishing—I didn't really think it mattered what it was."

"Abstinence is the enemy of love," misquoted Thrudd in agreement.

At the entrance they came face to face with Delphick. The Oracle eyed Miss Seeton accusingly.

"Since when have you started sticking pins into people?"

Miss Seeton colored. "It wasn't pins, Chief Superintendent, or not in that sense. It was a hatpin—and only the one. And," she added with a flash of spirit, "though not, of course, a thing one would choose to do in the ordinary way, I do feel, in this instance, it was justified. Besides, it kept saying so on all the buildings."

Used as Delphick was to Miss Seeton's wayward explanations, this last defeated him. "What buildings said what?"

"Why, 'Take Courage,' of course," she told him, "and it said it was the answer. So I did and it was. The answer, that is. I really couldn't have foreseen," she pointed out, "that it would explode—the gun, I mean—and that the car would go into a shop."

Delphick shook his head to clear it, while Thrudd murmured, "MissEss rides again."

"It's too late for you to go home," the chief superintendent decided. "We'll have to think of somewhere to put you for the night."

"Miss S. can doss down with me," said Mel. "I've got a spare bed."

Delphick thought it over. "Right. But I'll have to put a man on guard at your flat—just in case. And Miss Kenharding." He looked around. "Where is she?"

Thrudd grinned. "Hand in hand with Haley on a roseate cloud above a table, with waiters trying to reach up and feed 'em."

"Food!" exclaimed Mel. "Miss S. hasn't eaten. What about you?"

The chief superintendent realized that, with travel and worry, he'd had no food either; he was hungry. After arranging to station men at both Deirdre's and Mel's flats, he was easily persuaded to repair to the dining room with Miss Seeton and the two reporters, where payment for an excellent meal would, he knew, be exacted. He would be expected to supply details of the afternoon's—and the night's—events, but in fairness to Mel and Thrudd, he could not grudge them a scoop on information that would soon be public property. His main concern was Thatcher. Whether or not the syndicate made another attempt on Miss Kenharding, Miss Seeton, in her own inimitable way, had made fools of them. This Thatcher could not afford to allow and he would be bound, by the rules of his game, to eliminate her.

Thatcher's present bent was cold ferocity. The abduction of Deirdre Kenharding, with its inherent bargaining power, would have succeeded had it not been for the intervention of Miss Seeton. In all, this woman, this apparent simpleton, had now run rings round him and made him a laughingstock on four separate occasions.

To rule through fear presupposes that people are afraid and the fear must remain constant. All opposition must be overwhelmed; any failure in obedience must be punished. No dictator, in his own field, can afford to have his authority questioned, since the beginning of doubt is the seed of revolution, which flourishes in the compost of envy and hatred. More dangerous still is mockery; derision can crack the foundation of an empire.

Miss Seeton had offended on all counts and these

humiliations required that Thatcher's version of justice must not only be done but must be seen to be done.

He had his own sources of information and although he had not yet discovered the identity of the culprit, he knew that the police had been warned in advance of the attack at the Plummergen fête. This first sign of rebellion in the ranks a month ago would have been unthinkable: also, other members of the hierarchy in the syndicate would be glad to topple him from his position should it prove to their advantage. All in all, he recognized the situation demanded a gesture, an audacious gesture. He would prove that he did not depend on hired assassins. He could deal with such a situation, when need arose, far more effectively. It was essential that both the over- and the underworld should be aware who had killed the woman—and why. It was equally necessary that guilt should be impossible to prove. Such an action would atone for recent reversals, would reinstate him in his own and others' eyes and would put back fear where fear belonged.

Thatcher planned. . . . On her home ground—in her own cottage—with maximum publicity—his own presence in the vicinity known but accounted for, and connection with the event not susceptible to proof. Choose a moment when she was out, then when she returned . . . Thatcher planned—and Thatcher was pleased with his plan.

It was extraordinary, reflected Miss Seeton, how high up one appeared to be. When watching other people on bicycles, it didn't look like that at all, but once one was in the saddle oneself the ground did seem so unexpectedly far away. How very kind of Lady Colveden, who had a meeting and would not be back until later, to borrow Sir George's estate wagon and give her and her machine a lift into Brettenden, dropping her off at the bank for the interview which the bank manager had requested. To cycle to the town, although less than six miles, meant walking up this long hill, but to return, as she was now doing, was an entirely different matter. For this part of the journey one didn't have to use the pedals at all—just free-wheel. In Miss

Seeton's hands the wheel was rather freer than is customary and she weaved down the hill at an ever-increasing speed.

Such a relief, at the bank, to find it wasn't, as she had feared, that she hadn't enough, but that she had, in the manager's opinion, rather too much and ought to invest. What a difference doing drawings for the police had made to her life. And how grateful she felt. Invest? Now, in regard to this she wasn't sure. From what one read, investments always went down. And if there was income the government took most of that; if indeed, also from what one read, they didn't take over the shares as well. Surely she would do better to invest in labor-saving devices for the cottage, as Martha was always suggesting she should do. Then at least one could be sure of some return for one's outlay in less work and added comfort.

Behind Miss Seeton a car sounded its horn. She turned and waved a hand in apology, mounted the grass shoulder, swerved back onto the road, squeezed a handle which she assumed operated the brakes, but the bicycle, freed from the restriction of its gear lever, sped faster than before while the car, its driver deciding that discretion was the better part of road safety, crawled in her wake, continuing to play tortoise to Miss Seeton's hare.

Across the marsh Miss Seeton pedaled in a daydream of electric blankets, washing machines and automatic mixers, up into the village, to wobble down the Street in perfect time—how right she had been, for instance, to invest in a bicycle now that they only ran one bus a week to Brettenden—in perfect time for lunch.

Martha Bloomer met her at the door. "A man came."

"A man?" Miss Seeton could think of no stranger who was likely to call upon her.

"Well," admitted Martha grudgingly, "if he hadn't been foreign I'd've said he was a gentleman. Tall and wears glasses with one of those little beards and mustaches and he said he'd met you on the continent and that he owed you something and how sorry he was you weren't in but he left you this little parcel."

Miss Seeton eyed the brown-wrapped package dubiously.

Met on the Continent? Mr. Stemkos, whom she'd met in Switzerland? But no, Mr. Stemkos was clean-shaven. How very odd. "Who," she wondered, "could it be?"

"Well," said Martha, "he were over at the George and Dragon, his car was outside, and it were still there when I went over home five minutes ago, so I s'pect he's having dinner there."

A foreigner. And to leave a present for her . . . How very, very kind. But who, Miss Seeton still pondered, could it be?

Thatcher was pleased. Everything had worked out better than he might have hoped. The local pub—always the best source of information—had revealed that a Lady Something had given Miss Seeton a lift that morning to the nearest town and would not be back until midafternoon. Ideal. His own people would know—and the police might suspect—who the "foreign gentleman" had been, but they could prove nothing. Five men were prepared to swear him an alibi in London. Meanwhile he could afford to relax, have a leisurely lunch, which would allay suspicion, take a long route back to town; and before he arrived there, the balloon would have gone up. No possible connection with himself, and his aim—plus his object lesson to others—accomplished. No question, Thatcher felt, that he had reason to be pleased.

Delphick telephoned his sergeant at Plummergen, sent an urgent message to Brinton at Ashford, ordered a car and told his driver to burn tire rubber down to Kent. The informer had come through again: a bomb was being planted in Miss Seeton's cottage.

Bob Ranger forced an unwilling Miss Seeton to leave the weeding of a rose bed, put her in the charge of his wife, Anne, while he joined the local man, Potter, and the Ashford contingent in the search of Sweetbriars. All the adjacent houses, including an indignant Martha's—what about the family's tea?—had been evacuated and the excited villagers thronged behind the police cordon, as close as they could get to where the expected explosion should take place.

Sirens sounded continuously as more police arrived. The army bomb-disposal unit was already in attendance and in the midst of the commotion Delphick's car swept down the Street. He jumped out and hurried to confer with Brinton and Bob Ranger.

Miss Seeton caught his arm. "Chief Superintendent, please, what is all this? What's happened?"

"A bomb," the Oracle replied. "They've planted a time bomb in your cottage. We've got to—"

"A bomb?" She was incredulous. "A bomb? In my cottage? But that's ridiculous. Why should they? And who are 'they'?"

It dawned on Delphick that nobody had thought to question her. "Tell me—what's happened to you since this morning?"

"Why, nothing." Miss Seeton realized it was an official question and she must be accurate. "That is to say, I went to the bank—so very kind of Lady Colveden to give me a lift—and bicycled back. That is to say, I did. She couldn't, of course, because she had a meeting. And, naturally, no bicycle."

"And there was the man—the foreigner," chimed in Martha.

"Man? What foreigner?" demanded Delphick.

"Well, actually, he wasn't," explained Miss Seeton. "A foreigner, I mean. It was only Mr. Thatcher in a beard."

Delphick started to feel the familiar dreamlike quality which questioning her invariably entailed. He tried to take it slow. "Thatcher? Here? Are you sure?"

"Oh, yes," she replied. "He'd grown a beard and mustache, but, naturally, that doesn't alter the bones, the ears and eye sockets."

"Naturally not." He fought to be patient. "What was he doing?"

"Paying for his lunch, I imagine."

"You see"—Martha was determined to add her quota—"he'd left this parcel for Miss Emily—"

"Parcel?" Delphick rapped. "What parcel? Where is it?"

"On the little table in the passage—" began Martha.

"And she gave it to me—Martha, I mean," clarified Miss Seeton, "and said that he said he owed it to me and that he'd met me abroad, so I thought of Mr. Stemkos, which it couldn't be because of the beard, which he hadn't. Mr. Stemkos, that is."

"What?" Delphick tried not to shout.

Martha overrode him. "I'd told her his car was at the George and Dragon so—"

"So naturally," Miss Seeton took him up, "since one cannot, obviously, accept presents from gentlemen one does not know, I went there and he was going back. Back into the hotel, I mean, and had left the door open. The door of his car, that is, so that it seemed the best way, really. And so much less embarrassing."

Delphick gave up the unequal struggle with his feelings. *"What,"* he grated, *"did you do with the parcel?"*

Miss Seeton stared at him, nonplused. "Oh, but I thought I'd made it clear, Chief Superintendent. I put it on the floor behind his seat."